PIECE OF CAKE

DARA GIRARD

ISBN: 978-1949764475

PIECE OF CAKE

Published by ILORI Press Books

Cover Design and Layout Copyright © 2020 ILORI Press Books

Cover design by ILORI Press Books

Cover image copyright © Anna Pustynnikova/shutterstock

ILORI PRESS BOOKS, LLC

P.O. Box 10332

Silver Spring, MD 20914

www.iloripressbooks.com

Duvall Sisters

The Glass Slipper Project

Taming Mariella

A Reluctant Hero

The Black Stockings Society

Power Play

A Gentleman's Offer

Body Chemistry

Round the Clock

Return of the Black Stockings Society

Playing for Keeps

After Hours

A Private Affair

Just One Look

Private Lessons

The Main Attraction

Ladies of the Pen

Words of Seduction

Pages of Passion

Beneath the Covers

Henson Series

Table for Two

Gaining Interest

Careless Rapture

Dangerous Curves

Familiar Stranger

It Happened One Wedding

Unexpected Pleasure

Midnight Promise

Sweet Temptation

Always and Forever

Truly Yours

Say Yes

Clifton Sisters

The Sapphire Pendant

The Amber Stone

The Emerald Ring

Fortune Brothers

A Tempting Proposal

A Seductive Arrangement

An Unforgettable Moment

Novels

Honest Betrayal

The Daughters of Winston Barnett

Remember My Name

Illusive Flame

Winterwood Lane

Promise Me

This Changes Everything

Sparks

PART I

"**Beginnings are always messy.**"
John Galsworthy

CHAPTER ONE

The letter arrived like a tiny bomb.

But the elegant four level colonial home and the six bedrooms and seven baths it contained didn't shake or tremble. The expansive wraparound porch, painted a delicate cream that complemented the soft blue of the home's exterior, continued to gaze with arrogant splendor over the sea of roses, expertly trimmed bushes and soft carpet of lush green grass, which was tenderly cared for by the family's groundskeeper.

Not a tremor touched the wide front and back foyer, the sun filled family room, the cathedral ceilings on the top floor; nor did a single ball on the pool table roll a centimeter in the game room. Even the fully furnished lower level, where the media room and theatrical equipment sat ready to entertain at a moment's notice, barely felt a fissure of discord.

But discord had arrived in a thin, white envelope placed delicately on the side table in the foyer by the housekeeper. Few letters arrived at the house anymore. Holiday cards and junk mail mostly so little notice was given to the invader.

Although battered, it was a little crumpled as if it had been briefly held tightly in someone's fist, and there was a tiny rust-colored stain on the corner of the envelope, the letter hadn't traveled far to its destination.

Not as far as some of the other mail that arrived during the holidays making their journey from England, Jamaica, France, South Africa. This letter had only traveled one state away from Virginia Beach, Virginia to make its way to the desirable Maryland zip code of Brandon, a community that was only a few feet away from a vibrant downtown and metro station.

When Lauren Parker arrived home that cool April afternoon after a visit to her hairdresser, (who talked too much and never listened to how Lauren wanted her hair trimmed, but since the chatty woman was close enough to where Lauren liked to get her nails done Lauren didn't want the hassle of finding someone new she stayed and endured), she patted her brown Yorkie, Titi, picked up the mail and shifted through it, pleased that she had a moment of quiet before her daughters arrived home from dance class.

She paused at the sight of the envelope. At first scrunching her nose at the sight of it, wondering if she should complain to the post office about how they handled their mail. Imagine anyone seeing such a shabby object arriving at their doorstep—how unbecoming. But when she saw who had posted the letter, her irritation shifted to surprise. The letter was from Isabel.

Isabel. A sister she hadn't heard from in more than ten years.

However, Lauren was not a woman of rash actions or decisions. Although the letter shocked her, she was not eager to read its contents. She sighed and lifted the handle of the mother of pearl letter opener lying on the table but then became distracted when an overhead light bulb flickered and she realized it needed to be replaced. She made a mental note to remind her husband to tell the housekeeper. He was better at things like that. She didn't feel comfortable giving orders and he did it so well. Then her cell phone rang, she couldn't ignore a call from the president of the PTA, which would be bad manners, so she set the letter aside.

She remembered the letter again nearly twenty minutes later when she ended her call in the family room, she stood to retrieve it from the hallway but then got distracted by the sight of a handsome man on TV. She'd turned it on while pretending to listen to what the PTA president was proposing. The man on TV was rushing to a woman who was heading to board a ship. She just wanted to know what would happen next. Would he reach her? Would he miss his chance? Did the woman know he was there? The film that was so engrossing, a tragic romance, left her in tears nearly ninety minutes later. She loved a good cry.

So it wasn't until her husband came into the room, waving the unopened letter and commenting on it that Lauren finally took the time to do something with it. Like read it.

The beautiful handwriting on the lined, but cheap,

white paper made up for the letter's shabby exterior. The carefully written document took Lauren back in time and made her pulse quicken.

Isabel always had such lovely penmanship. Everyone thought so. Not that such a skill had much use nowadays. But the sight of the lovely handwritten letter shattered the silence that had come between them for more than a decade. A silence from her younger sister that she'd been prepared to live with, since their argument. Since Isabel had run off with a charming musician with little education, no money and a family that had disowned him. A man everyone had told her to stay away from.

Sonia, who had married a year after Lauren, and was adjusting to life in a small New York town with her husband, had tried to reason with Isabel, but both being passionate people, a violent argument erupted and Sonia vowed to never speak to Isabel again.

Lauren, desperate to get her sisters to reconcile, if not for their sakes for the sake of the family, had scolded her, in the most gentle of ways, to not break their parents' heart, but Isabel's harsh words—calling Lauren a snob because she'd married a well established man their Jamaican born parents could boast about; making fun of her elaborate wedding as a way to show off her "prized catch"—wounded her so deeply she decided not to interfere in Isabel's life again.

Lauren heard the front door open and close and nearly became distracted again when she heard the quick patter of her daughters race up to their bedrooms and then the no-nonsense heavy gait of her older sister, Sonia, as she headed down the hall. Sonia lived with them now after the unexpected death of her husband, a pastor, who'd gone to visit a church member and been mistaken for the woman's lover and been shot by the woman's jealous husband.

Lauren always wondered why her brother-in-law had been shot in the bedroom of the woman's ten year old son, wearing only a pair of briefs, and how a harmless trace of white sugar on his trousers could be mistaken for cocaine, but she was certain there was an innocent conclusion Sonia hadn't told her yet.

That unfortunate event had happened four years ago. Her sister had been very distraught and didn't want to stay alone in the house she used to share with her husband, so Lauren quickly made room for her on the first level of her house.

It was supposed to be temporary, but somehow had turned permanent. But Lauren didn't mind. She didn't like the thought of her sister on her own. She was a great help to them around the house, managing the house-keeper, groundskeeper and her two daughters better than Lauren ever could, giving her enough time to devote to taking care of herself.

How she presented herself was key to being the successful wife of a top medical researcher and business owner, she was on the board of a charity, which, thank-fully, only met twice a year, entertained guests for her husband and hosted birthday parties for her daughters. However, she did let Sonia do most of the planning and arranging of these events too, since she was a woman with many opinions. Lauren couldn't imagine being without her. Her sister could be a bit bossy sometimes, but

Lauren had learned never to go against someone who regularly thought God was on their side.

"What do you have there?" Sonia asked taking a seat. She was a stocky, handsome woman with high cheekbones, the same roasted almond skin tone she shared with her two sisters and piercing dark eyes. She pinned them on Lauren making goosebumps skitter along her arms. For some reason her sister made her feel as if she were in trouble even if she wasn't.

"It's a letter."

"I can see it's a letter," she said with impatience. "Who's it from?"

Lauren took a deep breath; her sister was always in a hurry for some reason. She didn't understand the rush, the letter wasn't going anywhere. Lauren counted to three and when she spoke she made sure to keep her voice pleasant. No reason to sound annoyed. "Isabel."

Sonia stared at her in shock. A shock that Lauren would have also felt if she'd possessed her sister's strong feelings. Sonia always felt things at a higher level; Lauren didn't have the energy. Sonia had made a good pastor's wife, rallying the congregation into a united force when needed and calming their fears too, especially after the death of her husband. "Are you sure?"

"Of course I'm sure. Her name is right here." She waited for her sister's temper to flash, but released a breath of relief when she realized there was no anger in her eyes. Clearly time and God had mellowed Sonia's opinion of their sister.

"What does she say?"

"I recognized the handwriting, but haven't had a

chance to read it yet."

"Why not? Let me see." Sonia snatched the letter from her and Lauren sighed again, not having the energy to fight her. She watched her sister's sharp brown gaze quickly sweep over the words; her hands shift through the sheets of paper. There seemed to be so many of them. Oh dear, why did Isabel have to be so wordy? After a few minutes of silence her curiosity could take no more and Lauren said, "Well, what is it?"

Sonia rested the letter on the sofa face down, her face pained. "Our dear sister is in a bad way."

Lauren stiffened. She hoped it wasn't bad news. She really didn't want to hear bad news. It had been so long, she had hoped Isabel had come to her senses and wanted to see them again. A letter of apology would have been so much better. Lauren cleared her throat and braced herself. "If it's bad news, tell it to me quickly. Has her husband left her?"

Sonia sniffed. "She'd be so lucky. She's on her seventh."

"Husband?"

"No, child. She evidently doesn't know how condoms work. She's scheduled to pop in July."

Lauren curled her lip in distaste. Sonia hadn't had children yet (and didn't seem in a hurry to do so) and while Lauren would never point that out to her, she was keenly aware of how uncomfortable she'd felt the last two months of her last pregnancy. The first pregnancy had been so easy, almost blissful; the second still made her shudder, so she didn't like the description. "That's a horrible turn of phrase. Did she say it like that?"

"No."

"I prefer you not paraphrase things in such a coarse way. So she's expecting her seventh child?"

"Hmm."

She was amazed her sister had both the energy and stamina. "Does she know what it will be?"

"Does it matter?"

Lauren sighed. "I suppose not." Although she was curious. While she did enjoy her two girls, it would have been nice to have had them evenly split: One boy and one girl. The family photos would have been lovely when she sent them out every Christmas. A boy as handsome as his father would have been a nice addition, but it wasn't to be. "You said she's in a bad way."

"Yes."

"Does she need something?"

"She needs everything," Sonia said stressing the word. "Her useless husband is of no help."

"He can't be that useless if he's blessed her with nearly seven children."

Sonia shook her head. "God blesses." She pointed to the ceiling. "It is His mighty hand of favor that washes over us and allows us to multiply. Man is but a lowly creature used as a vehicle, raised from the—"

"Yes, yes," Lauren cut in. She was in no mood to hear about God's greatness and the weaknesses of mankind. She waved a dismissive hand. "Wrong choice of words, you know what I mean. I think you're being unfair. Did Isabel call him useless?" Lauren reached out her hand to see the letter.

Sonia rested her hand on top of it, as if resting her

hand on a sacred text, her fingers spread out giving Lauren a chance to appreciate her French manicure. "I'm reading between the lines. She still thinks he's as wonderful as ever, but he hasn't been able to work."

"Why can't he work? I thought he was a musician."

"Not anymore. He's in construction now. Or at least was before he was supposedly forced to stop after an on-site work injury seven years ago."

Lauren tapped her chin, pensive. "There's that number again. Seven. Seven children, seven years ago. I wonder if it means anything."

"It means that our dear sister is in need of our help."

"I'll send baby clothes."

"No, she wants to send one of her children."

"Where?"

"Here."

Lauren's brows shot up. She held out her hand again. "Let me see the letter."

Sonia lifted the letter and began to read it again. "She says she has a bright girl of..." Sonia stopped.

"What?"

"Don't say it. When I tell you the girl's age don't read anything more into it. It's not of a concern."

"I won't."

"She's a girl of seven."

"Seven again?"

"...who could do with a chance at a better education," Sonia continued to read. She set the letter down on her lap. "Poor Isabel really doesn't have the energy to look after her. She says she already has another daughter who is doing well with an aunt of ours."

Lauren frowned. "A little girl. I'm not sure I want another little girl. Perhaps a boy."

"I think it's a great idea," Sonia said. "We should help out in any way we can. We must forget the past and move forward. It's our God-given duty."

"I'll have to ask Timothy."

"I'm sure he'll agree."

And being the type of woman she was Sonia was determined to make sure he did.

At first he was reluctant.

"Wouldn't the child be homesick so far away from her family?" he asked at dinner. A succulent meal of jerk chicken and yellow rice: his favorite. It had been prepared as if to put him in a good mood. He was in a very good mood. His daughters had left the dinner table early leaving the adults to discuss in private. Usually his youngest daughter would grumble and the other would ask what was for dessert before dinner was served, Sonia would scold her then there would be pouting or tears.

But not tonight.

Tonight the two women set out to put Timothy in the best mood possible.

"Children are resilient," Sonia said, "and I think it's our duty to help our poor sister out."

Timothy looked at his wife. He made a token attempt to disagree with her sister, but within five minutes surrendered and agreed that it was a good idea.

And that was how Cirina "Rina" Powell came to live with the Parkers of Brandon, Maryland and changed their lives forever.

CHAPTER TWO

Sonia didn't know exactly what she was expecting when the child finally arrived at the house.

Her brother-in-law had gone to pick her up and Sonia had busied herself, making sure that the room on the fourth floor was as close to perfect as possible. Although she knew true perfection was God's dominion and it was man's hubris to even try to rise and attain such a level, she still let herself indulge.

The upper level room was not as grand as any of the rooms on the bedroom level, nor as elegant as the guest room, but it was suitable.

She thought about Isabel's daughter as she instructed the housekeeper on the color of the bedspread and the location of the pillows. Unfortunately, Lauren had gone a bit overboard with toys and dolls and they crowded the bed and shelves. Sonia didn't think Isabel's daughter should be ruined by spoiling; one brought up as she must have for the past seven years wasn't accustomed to the material pleasures her cousins had grown used to, so she left one large teddy bear to sit in the corner of the room and took the rest of the toys away. She planned to donate most of them to a local shelter for women and children where they would be better served.

She never had a clear picture in her mind of what Isabel's daughter would look like, but as she looked at her now, she knew *this* wasn't it.

The image before her was that of a small, thin creature with angular features and plaited black hair. Sonia studied Isabel's daughter as the girl slowly walked into the family room wearing a dress that had been washed so often, that the flower pattern could barely be seen anymore. It had likely been yellow at one point but now looked an ugly light brownish-white.

Sonia pushed down her disappointment. She had been eager to see and possibly dote on a miniature version of Isabel.

Isabel who'd been a little reckless, pretty and daring, but always lovable.

There was nothing to love about this child. The child looked nothing like her sister. She lacked her sister's shining eyes and sweet round face. She had all the useless features of her father. A chin that was a shade too long and haughty. She had dark eyes, rather than Isabel's light brown eyes she fondly remembered, and a mouth that turned down at the corners. Handsome but not pretty. Sonia liked pretty things. She believed God did too. He wouldn't have made the mountains and the trees if He hadn't.

She instantly felt her heart grow cold against the child. She saw arrogance and shiftiness, if this child wasn't kept in her place she would take advantage of them just like Isabel's husband had of her sister. Sonia wouldn't allow that.

She was keen to make sure no serpent entered their Eden.

Lauren saw Isabel's daughter in a different way as the child walked into the family room and stood before them. Lauren was so pleased the child was quiet. Her dear loves, Carla and Amelia, could be so noisy and boisterous sometimes, squealing with delight in a way that would give her a headache. This was a child who didn't look like a squealer, which was a plus. And she didn't look like she'd eat much either. Perhaps she'd be a good example to Amelia who liked to hide sweets and could never resist a pastry.

She didn't smell. That was a relief as well. She smelled like cheap soap, but at least she was clean. Lauren had worried about the child's hygiene but now realized she shouldn't have. Her sister had been properly raised. She may have married poorly, but thankfully certain standards had been maintained.

Four year old Carla didn't find the newcomer particularly interesting, (especially since she still hadn't gotten the kitten she'd asked for), and neither did her six year old sister, Amelia, who wondered why her cousin only had one suitcase.

"Is her room ready?" Timothy asked.

"Of course it is," Sonia said in a sharp tone, both

surprised and offended her brother-in-law would even think she would be behind schedule.

Timothy nodded, taking no notice of her tone, and said, "Then let me show it to her. I think she needs to rest." He reached down and took the girl's hand, unnerved by how small and thin it felt in his own, and the child looked up at him, briefly uncertain and surprised by the gesture. "Come on," he said and she tightened her grip a fraction around his and humbly followed.

CHAPTER THREE

"Am I being punished?"

Timothy looked down at the child surprised. "Of course not."

But Rina wasn't so sure. The room was so large and quiet and far from everyone else, high on the top floor of this large house. Like a tower. She knew towers were where bad people were sent.

At home, when anyone got into trouble, they were tied up in the boiler room in the basement of the apartment complex. Mom said it was to keep them safe and she believed her. Two years ago, her little brother had wandered off and gotten hit by a motorcycle, he'd never been the same since. He only blinks and stares into the distance and doesn't speak.

But everyone knew the basement was punishment because you were always tied up and left there by yourself. All alone.

All alone among the moan of pipes, the scurrying of rat's feet, the smell of dampness.

She hated being alone. Once, when she'd gotten punished for losing the five dollars she was to use to buy milk and cheese at the convenience store (she'd put it in her pocket before realizing her jeans' pocket had a large hole), she'd been tied to the railing as usual, but then Dad forgot about her.

She'd been alone there, in that musky boiler room, for an entire day when she heard giggling and sucking noises.

Rina called out, her voice hoarse from shouting, and heard someone swear. Then a teenage girl peeked her head around the corner, stared at her for a moment; the guy with her stuck his head around seconds later, clearly feeling it was safe to reveal himself as well. They both walked up to her. The brown-skinned girl with long braids and big hoop earrings wore a Boys II Men T-shirt and torn jeans; the boy was gangly with the attempts of a mustache on his upper lip and a T-shirt with a picture of Beavis and Butt-Head.

"What are you doing down here?" the girl said.

"I got punished."

"And you smell like piss too."

Rina felt her face burn. She'd wet herself, although she'd tried to get herself loose.

"Why'd you stay down here? The door's not locked."

"I know." Rina looked at her wrists. "But I couldn't untie the knot."

The girl swore and rushed to untie her; the boy just stared at her. "Do you know where you live?" she asked. "Should I call someone?"

Rina rubbed her wrists once they were freed. "No, I'm fine. Thanks."

"Should we call the police or something?" she heard the boy whisper.

Rina felt her body tremble. Was this part of her punishment? Had her father told them what had happened? Did he still think she'd stolen the money? "I really didn't steal the five dollars. I lost it." She pulled out the interior of the pocket with the hole as she had done to show her father, hoping they'd believe her. "Truly. I can go back over where I went and—"

The girl rested a hand on her shoulder. "It's okay." She looked at her friend. "Stop scaring her."

The boy frowned. "I wasn't tryin' to. I just thought..."

Rina felt tears build. "I didn't mean to—"

The girl patted her shoulder. "No, no we wouldn't call the police on you. You're not in trouble."

Rina frowned confused. "Then why would you call them?"

The two teenagers looked at each other. "Leave it alone," the girl said when the boy opened his mouth. "We shouldn't get involved." She pulled out her purse and took out some money. "Here."

Rina stared at the ten dollars the girl had given her. "I don't have change."

"Girl, I don't need change." She waved it insistent. "It's yours."

She took it. "Really?"

"Yes, now go straight home."

Rina folded up the ten dollar bill and stuck it in her

sock. Now she could buy what her family needed and keep a little for herself. The thought made her happy.

She left the boiler room and headed for the elevators, but they weren't working again, so she had to walk up the four flights of stairs to her apartment. Past the door with music playing so loud she could feel the drumbeat in her chest, past the door where a couple was shouting dirty words at each other with laughter in their voice— "You're such an a*hole." "B*tch you know you love me."—past the door where savory smells of roasted potatoes and butter biscuits, drifted into the hallway.

She usually lingered there, imagining what the lucky family was having for dinner, but this time Rina knew she had to get home. If she hadn't wet herself, she would have taken the money to the store right away, but she didn't want anyone to see her like this.

She reluctantly made her way down the hall to the door where she heard a TV blaring, a baby crying and something big and metal clattering to the ground. Probably her older sister, Jenny, in the kitchen, she always managed to drop something.

Rina stopped in front of the door and knocked. She heard another clatter then Jenny let her in. Among the noise of her siblings, one sat in front of the TV gripping a teddy bear Rina had found in the hallway. She patted her three year old brother on the head as he sat and blinked at the wall, she gave the youngest his pacifier that had fallen out of reach of his playpen. She heard her father snoring in another room and saw her mother lying on the couch with a CD player and headphones on her round belly as she watched something on TV. Her newly ironed *Home and More* work shirt hung on the back of the couch. Her mother shifted her pretty brown gaze then straightened a little when she saw her. "Where are you coming from? Where have you been?"

"Dad forgot me in the basement," Rina said in a tight voice. She stood still, hoping that her mother wouldn't notice the tiny bulge in her sock.

Her mother motioned her forward, Rina's pulse quickened. What did she want? Did she think she was lying?

When Rina was within arm's reach, her mother lightly patted her cheek with tender but rough hands and said, "I'm sure he didn't mean it. Remember to behave better next time. Now go wash up and get something to eat."

There wasn't much left to eat. Bread and jam would do.

She sat at the table and took a deep breath as she stared at the brown bread covered in grape jelly. She wanted to make it last so she ate it very slowly. It was something she'd taught herself to do at five years old. She learned to make a slice of bread last an entire sitcom. As her mother laughed, she'd take a bite. She later learned that was a whole thirty minutes. One day she'd make a slice of bread last an hour, but she hadn't been able to do that yet. Sometimes she pretended to be a ghost and imagined no one saw her—just the bread as it slowly disappeared in tiny bites. The image amused her.

After she finished eating, she went to the convenience store and bought the cheese and milk her mother had wanted, but no one noticed them in the fridge. Or at least no one asked where they had come from. She bought a small bag of cheese sticks for herself, because they were easy to open without anyone hearing the plastic.

But she preferred cheese popcorn. She also liked to lick the inside of potato chip packets she'd get from school. Her friends thought she was strange because she'd always ask them for their empty packets; she'd stash them away in her backpack and then take them home and cut them up for her family. Her brothers liked the salt and pepper chip bags, two sisters liked the sour cream chip bags, another barbecue (before she was sent to live with a great-aunt), Rina preferred cheese. The cheesier the better and she didn't care which kind: cheese crackers or popcorn or puffs, although she'd learned that the cheese puffs left the cheesiest orange powder behind. She had to hide her stash, carefully stretching it out over days or it wouldn't last. She didn't mind sharing; it was seeing it all gone that hurt the most, she liked things to last.

But at least she wasn't alone back then.

But here, in this grand house, she was. It was so quiet and clean.

She didn't want to be alone in this big room by herself. Being alone meant punishment. Why were they punishing her?

"No, this is all yours," her uncle said. "You can have your own room now."

She looked up at her uncle. He smiled. He didn't look like someone who would lie. She liked his mustache and the big silver colored watch on his wrist. He acted as if he were giving her a special gift. She didn't want to disappoint him. "Thank you."

"You're welcome." He started to set her suitcase on the bed, but before he could the handle broke and the suitcase fell to the ground splitting open and scattering her clothes on the floor and her secret stash of chips and cracker packets, which floated through the air like dried leaves in autumn.

Her uncle stared. "What in the world?"

Rina rushed forward and quickly began gathering them, stuffing them back in her suitcase. There had been eight of them. She'd counted. "I'm so sorry," she said.

"It's okay. It's not your fault. But why—?"

She didn't want him to think she'd cause trouble, so she quickly said, "I'll do it," when he bent down to help her pick up her things.

"Honey, if it's garbage you don't have to put it back in your suitcase. You have a trashbin over there." He pointed.

It wasn't garbage. "Okay," she said taking a green shirt and covering her treasure.

He stared at her for a long moment and she wondered if she'd made him angry. "I'll clean it all up," she added. "I'll be clean. I promise."

"Don't be afraid to ask for help."

She didn't need help and didn't understand why he'd think she'd be afraid of that. He was a strange man. "Okay."

He patted her on the shoulder. It was a strange sensation. No one had ever patted her like that before. Her mother liked to pat her cheek when she thought Rina was upset, and her father sometimes gave her a hard whack on the bottom when he thought she was being sassy, but never this strange heavy hand on her shoulder. It felt comforting somehow. "Get some rest," he said before he left and closed the door.

Rina ran forward and grabbed the doorknob. When she touched it, the knob turned easily in her hand. The door wasn't locked. She swung the door open. Her tension eased.

Her uncle paused and turned to her. "Did you want something?"

She didn't know if she should tell him about how her mother would sometimes lock them in their room when her Dad's friends came by. Once, one of his friends got so drunk he ended up in the bed Rina shared with her siblings.

He fell on top of her, slick and wet like a seal, and she'd screamed and pushed him off. He'd stumbled back and fell on the ground and passed out. He reminded her of a fallen scarecrow with his limbs sprawled on the ground. They all thought it was funny, but her mother never laughed about it. Since then her mother didn't mention the incident and would be careful about locking the door. If her mother didn't think that story was funny her uncle might not either. "No, nothing."

He smiled and Rina briefly wondered if he were truly as nice as he looked. She wanted him to like her. She waved and he waved back then disappeared down the stairs.

Leaving her all alone to wonder why her parents had really sent her away.

CHAPTER FOUR

*T*imothy didn't like returning to the family room without her. Twice he thought about taking his niece's hand and letting her be with them. But he also thought she needed space to adjust. Now he wasn't so sure.

His two daughters amused themselves with a cartoon on the TV, while his wife buffed her nails. His sister-in-law watched the screen with pursed lips. Either she'd found something unsuitable about the cartoon, which she would let them all know in no uncertain words, or something else was bothering her.

"Has she settled in?" Sonia asked the moment Timothy walked into the room.

He inwardly sighed. He preferred dealing with other challenges—managing his property holdings, investments and the work in his research lab—to dealing with people. It was moments like this when he wished he could lock himself away and disappear into the intricacy of a microbe. He had little interest in the drama family life brought. He felt providing for his family and being a steady presence should be enough. But more often than not it wasn't.

Timothy frowned as he took a seat. "There's something about that child that bothers me."

Sonia stiffened in her seat. "You sense it too? We must be on guard and vigilant against it."

His frowned deepened. "No, I didn't mean that she's a threat. I mean—"

"We must watch her carefully."

"I think she might have things she's not telling us." He hesitated wondering whether he should tell them about the trash in the suitcase. Why would she keep it?

Sonia's gaze sharpened, she leaned closer. "You sense deceit?"

No, telling Sonia wouldn't be helpful. He'd have to tread carefully. "No...I don't know how to put it into words. Like she's hiding something."

Sonia clicked her tongue in pity. "So young to already show signs of her father's wicked ways."

"No." He let his gaze shift to his daughters, regretting he'd said anything, but it was too late to back down now. "I don't think that's it. I'm not sure she should be up there by herself. She seems a little frightened."

Lauren opened her mouth to reply, but Sonia beat her to it. "It's perfect for her," she said, her tone adamant. "We need to keep the guest room free."

"But I don't think guests would mind it. She might feel more like family if she were on the third floor bedroom level with the rest of us."

Lauren delicately cleared her throat. "Perhaps we—"

"We don't want to force a relationship that isn't there yet," Sonia said. "She might feel overwhelmed."

"I think she already feels overwhelmed so—"

"A blessing like this would overwhelm anyone. Imagine how Joseph felt being let out of the dungeon to live in a mighty palace."

"I hardly think it's the same thing," Timothy said. "She's awfully young to have been sent by herself."

"She made it safely," Sonia said.

"Yes, but—"

"It builds character."

Timothy stroked his chin. "I'm not sure—"

"She will adjust," Sonia said then softened her tone. "Timothy you have such a kind heart. I made special consideration for her room. It has everything a little girl could possibly want."

Timothy glanced at his wife who gave him a barely perceived shake of the head. It wasn't worth arguing about. Letting Sonia have her way was the best option.

Peace was all that mattered.

CHAPTER FIVE

Rina hated being alone, but what she hated even more was being scared.

That night she was afraid. She was afraid of the dark and the silence that surrounded her. And the bear that looked as big as a man that sat in the corner of the room watching her. She imagined it opening its mouth ready to eat her. She didn't like the sound of the wind as it rushed past her window and the shadows the moon cast along the floor.

Rina scrambled out of bed and turned on the lights. But it didn't help. She was still alone and the large bear still watched her.

She left her room and waited for her eyes to grow accustomed to the dark before she walked down the stairs, and turned onto the hallway beneath her. She tried to remember what her uncle had told her about the third floor. Moonlight filtered up from the windows on the main floor, which made the corridor a little easier to see, but she was still confused.

He'd pointed and said that the room at the end of the hall was the main bedroom, she supposed that was where he and Aunt Lauren slept, then he'd pointed to three other rooms telling her they made up the guest bedroom, Clara's room and Amelia's room.

The problem was she didn't remember which one was which.

Rina took a deep breath and lightly knocked on the door closest to her.

When no one answered she cautiously opened the door and crept inside.

She heard a fury of motion coming from the bed, the crinkling of plastic and a mumbled voice say, "Who is it?"

"It's me," Rina said. She still couldn't tell whose room she'd snuck into, but she smelled a hint of chocolate and vanilla. "Can I turn on the lights?"

"No." She heard more movement she couldn't quite place, but it was food related. She could almost tell the different sounds of packages. Potato chip packages were a little different than cookie ones. If she guessed right, there were cookies being eaten somewhere. Chocolate chip and oatmeal raisin. "Not yet. What do you want?" her cousin asked sounding a little less muffled than before. She recognized her voice as her cousin Amelia. "Are you spying on me?"

Rina stood where she was not daring to go closer. "Why would I spy? What are you doing? Are you eating something?"

"Oh for goodness sakes." Rina felt rather than saw,

Amelia rush past her and close the door. "I'm not doing anything wrong."

"I didn't think you were. Can I turn on the lights now?"

Amelia released a heavy sighed. "Sure."

When light finally flooded the room, Rina blinked to adjust then noticed chocolate on her cousin's cheek and saw the gleam of a foil packet on the ground beside her bed.

Amelia folded her arms. She was pretty like Aunt Lauren with two thick braids that fell down her back and she wore a nightgown with unicorns printed on it.

"What do you want?"

"Can I stay with you?"

She narrowed her eyes. "Why? You've got your own room."

Rina hugged herself. "I'm afraid. I'm not used to sleeping by myself."

She sighed. "Promise not to say anything?"

Rina nodded.

Amelia studied her for a moment before she said, "Okay, then get in, silly."

Sleeping in the same bed with Amelia was heavenly. She smelled like sugar and chocolate and she was soft like a marshmallow. Rina would have stayed with Amelia every night if they hadn't gotten caught nearly three weeks later. She'd forgotten to wake up early enough to sneak back to her bedroom without anyone noticing. Instead, Carla had seen her coming out of Amelia's room and accused them of having fun without her and immediately told her mother.

Which led to Rina being sent to her room to stay there until told when to leave, followed by a discussion between the adults in the family room.

"She has her own room," Sonia said. "Why would she need to share one? Let alone a bed!"

"I told you I thought something was wrong," Timothy said. "This proves it."

"This proves that she's sneaky. The thought of her creeping around at night without any of us suspecting a thing. She has the makings of a burglar."

"That's a bit extreme."

"I think it's adorable," Lauren said. "It's like they were having their own private sleepover."

Sonia shivered. "Walking around without making a sound. Gives me chills."

"It's a new place," Timothy said. "It takes some adjusting. I see no harm in it."

"I think it is best that she starts to get used to the way we do things around here."

"But—"

"We must set rules and stick to them. We would only confuse her by letting her get her way. Children like that must be given strict guidelines to follow. I understand that the change from her home to here takes adjustment, but the change should be quick and swift."

And quick and swift it was. Rina was not allowed to go to Amelia's room again. Or anywhere else. Although she pleaded to even be allowed to sleep in the corner of her uncle and aunt's room. No begging moved them.

She cried.

Not where anyone could see her, but softly, alone in

her room.

She cried because of the darkness, and being alone in the bed made her miss home and miss the comfort of being with someone else.

She hugged her pillow and let the tears fall trying not to think about being left alone in the boiler room again. She wanted to be happy. Her mother had told her that her life would be better. She wanted to believe what her mother said. Her mother said that her other sister lived in a fine house with a kind woman. A great-aunt who'd had no children of her own. From the little notes and sketches her sister had sent them, Rina believed it.

Her mother had told her it would be the same for her. That was sort of true. Her aunts were just like her mother had described them. Aunt Lauren was pretty and always lying on the couch like her mother liked to do. It made Rina feel at home. Aunt Lauren was always asking her to get her things, like her mother used to do when a new baby was on the way.

She'd help her mother put on her socks and shoes and lotion her legs. Her mother would always tease her about not being able to see her feet. It was always how Rina knew she'd be getting a new sibling. Her mother would say, "My feet will disappear soon" and the image of her mother's feet fading away always made Rina giggle because she knew that people's feet didn't disappear. Her mother later explained that as her belly got bigger she couldn't see her feet anymore and that having a baby was a lot of work so Rina and the others had to be good to her if they loved her.

And she loved her mother very much so she did

whatever her mother told her. She'd go to the store and feed the others and change diapers and wash clothes. It was tiring, but baby after baby must be tiring too.

Rina sometimes wondered why her mother kept wanting to have babies but didn't think she had a right to ask. Her father didn't seem to care much for babies. He liked to spend time out with his friends. He couldn't do much after getting hurt at work, which happened the year she was born. Mom had been very worried about him when he'd ended up in the hospital she'd told her. They'd all worried about him for a couple years, until the man in the sharp grey suit who smelled like spearmint gum showed up and told her parents there was another way to get cheques without working and that the company owed him. The sharp suited man made her parents happy. And cheques did come, but they never seemed to be enough. And their lives weren't much better than before. Rina wondered about her father's guitar, which sat untouched in the corner of the living room and she wondered if he'd ever played it, although she'd once seen a picture of him holding it.

Her dad seemed to be happiest when he drank or left to be with his friends. His friends amused her. They were always funny.

They sometimes brought gifts too, like a bag of apples or oranges. But when they brought bottles Mom was never happy and her father's mood seemed to dim. He didn't laugh as much.

She always got a little nervous at the sound of cans or bottles clinking in a bag. She knew that wasn't good. Her mother liked to drink sometimes, but her mood always stayed the same. She stopped when her feet were going to disappear, but soon after would start again. Rina wondered what they both liked so much about drinking, but her mother said that she would know more when she was older.

But, fortunately, helping Aunt Lauren wasn't as hard as helping her mother. She didn't ask Rina for the same things. She asked for things Rina didn't know about. Things that she'd never heard of like a face mask, a strange jelly like object with cutout eyes, or a truffle. Plus, Rina was always sent to look for her slippers. Rina couldn't understand how her aunt could keep misplacing such fine items made of the softest fabric she'd ever felt. But when Rina had asked her what a breast lift was (she'd stumbled on the strange package when searching in her aunt's dresser drawer for the gloves she liked to put on her hands) her aunt frowned and told her to stop asking so many questions.

Aunt Lauren also had a dog, Titi, that at first Rina had thought was a cat. It was so small and its fur long and it barely moved. Her Aunt Lauren liked to carry it around with her and sometimes dressed it up. The dog didn't seem to mind.

Rina was once allowed to brush it and had felt very pleased at the responsibility. It was a lot easier than changing diapers.

Aunt Sonia was just as striking as her mother had said, with beautiful dark eyes. Rina tried to please her and asked to help in any way she could, but Aunt Sonia kept her distance. She was a woman always on the move. She couldn't seem to stay still. She was always in motion either talking to the people in the kitchen, or the people working on the lawn.

Rina couldn't understand why her aunts and uncle needed so many people to help them. There weren't that many of them, why couldn't Aunt Lauren or Uncle Timothy cook? But it seemed the way that things were done and she didn't want to complain.

She was happy she didn't have to hide food packets anymore. She liked Aunt Sonia, although she wasn't sure Aunt Sonia liked her very much. Her tone always changed when she spoke to her. It was like a soft, still lake when she spoke to Carla and Amelia but became a sheet of ice when she spoke to Rina and she had thoughts of falling through the sheet that covered her aunt's words and drowning in the icy waters beneath. But she would work her hardest to belong. To fit in.

She knew she couldn't be bubbly and adorable like Carla or clever and sweet like Amelia, but she could be helpful. That was what she was good at.

So when the family planned a trip to Hawaii that July Rina thought of all the things she could do to make them like her.

She packed her suitcase, her heart racing. Her first trip as a family. She'd never had one of those before. She'd heard about them. Other kids at school had talked about going on drives or flying in planes or riding on trains. She'd been on a bus, but only by herself. She'd never known what that was like and now they were going to Hawaii. She's learned that it was an island with volcanoes located in the Pacific Ocean.

"Where do you think you're going?"

Rina turned to see Aunt Sonia standing in her bedroom doorway, her arms folded.

She looked at her aunt confused. "I...I thought we were going to Hawaii."

"Yes, the *family*. Not you."

Tears tightened her throat and filled her eyes.

"I'm not family?"

"You're a relative. There is a distinction. They want time together without you. It's only natural."

Rina felt hot tears stream down her face. She thought she'd made them happy. She thought she finally would belong. But she'd failed. They didn't like her. They were going to leave her by herself in this big house. "You're leaving me here all alone?" Her voice cracked in misery.

Aunt Sonia bristled. "There's no need to cry. Of course not." She sighed. "I have to stay behind and look after you until next week."

"Next week?"

"Then you'll take a bus to spend time with *your* family and I'll fly to join my sister and *her* family." She clasped her hands together. "Isn't that great? Aren't you eager to see your parents again?"

Rina felt like there was a hidden meaning in her question, that there was only one answer and that answer had better be yes. She saw that although Aunt Sonia's eyes were beautiful, they were also very hard. "Yes," Rina said knowing that would please her.

Aunt Sonia allowed a faint smile. "That's what I thought."

SONIA LEFT HER NIECE'S ROOM WITH A FEELING OF triumph. It hadn't been easy to persuade Lauren and Timothy of the prudence of her suggestion but in the end Sonia had won out. "I don't think it's wise that she join you," she remembered instructing them late one afternoon while they sat on the porch while the children played in the garden. Well at least Carla and Amelia were playing, Rina, unfortunately, was distracting the gardener from his duty by asking him questions. "At least not yet. She can't forget her siblings and parents."

Lauren took a sip of lemonade then slowly set the glass down. "But nearly two months is a rather long time."

"You can send money with her. I'm sure Isabel misses her, although she'd never say so."

In truth, Sonia didn't feel that the child should ever forget where she came from. They shouldn't raise her like the other two. There had to be a distinction. Rina was not one they could spoil or coddle. If she wanted to save her soul from the bad blood she'd inherited this was the best way. She'd been sent to them for a reason, as a test.

Sonia didn't plan to fail.

It was better Rina be with her family over the summer and help them and stay where she belonged even if it was only a few months out of the year. She was too smart for her own good and could manipulate them.

While Sonia held a smug smile as she descended the stairs, Rina sat alone in her bedroom and stared at her suitcase. Bitter disappointment and shame gripped her as she wiped away her tears. Of course she should be happy to see her parents again. She loved her family. Then why didn't she want to go? Why did she wish that Aunt Lauren and Uncle Timothy were taking her with them too?

The two days before they left, Rina tried to be extra good and silently wished her aunt and uncle would change their minds and decide to take her with them. That one day at dinner Uncle Timothy would say with that kind smile of his, that she truly was family. That Aunt Lauren would call her over to the couch and whisper that she would love to have her go with them.

But that day never came.

They waved their goodbyes before they headed out the door and left her alone with Aunt Sonia. Despite all her hopes she didn't get to travel with them to Hawaii nor to Vancouver nor to Paris. Instead, she spent the next several summers in the cramped apartment with her parents and siblings for one week before being sent to stay with her maternal grandparents who'd returned to Jamaica to live out their retirement.

They were kind people and loved their children and grandchildren, but felt they'd earned the right to live their lives free of them so they brushed her off on their cook. A woman who also didn't have much use for a child, and found it irritating to have a child underfoot, so Rina spent hours finding ways to amuse herself. One of her favorite activities was walking along the beach, where she could look out at the ocean and not feel alone.

It was that first summer, when she was seven, that she met the man who would introduce her to a passion that would change the course of her life.

CHAPTER SIX

The last thing Charlie expected to see as he took a drag of the cigarette he'd told his wife he'd quit, was the silhouette of a kid walking alone on the beach, making its way past the row of palm trees as the sun slowly rose over the Caribbean Sea.

Among the four hundred acres of manicured grounds and two miles of beach front, the Star Moon Hotel and Resort boasted numerous suites and villas. Soon the hotel would burst with life as guests took pleasure in playing tennis, indulging in a spa oasis, horseback riding along the beach and a gourmet dining experience, for which he was partially responsible as the main pastry chef who supervised four others on his shift.

But at three in the morning the resort sounds were more muted. It was how he liked it. He always came early to work at the Star Moon Hotel and Resort so that he could enjoy a cigarette before he freshened up and entered the kitchen of the luxury resort. It was the one place where he felt completely himself.

A fourth generation Chinese-Jamaican, he never grew tired of the stretch of water that could gleam a pristine blue in the afternoon and turn an inky black in the evening, carrying with it the scent of coconut palms and a soft flower-scented breeze. He always enjoyed the early morning sun as it slowly rose over the water and the sand, the silhouette of palm trees, a dot of black of a chimney swift or yellow-billed cuckoo soaring through the sky. He'd grown used to the sight and could see it in his mind, but the kid was new.

And out of place.

From what he could see, the kid was as scrawny as a reed. It was too early for a child to be out on their own. It didn't matter that the well lit resort shone like a beacon in the early morning. Tourists and regulars could make a child disappear without warning.

Charlie took a long drag of his cigarette, exhaled slowly and waited for the kid to come closer to the palm tree where he stood. The child wore a baseball cap, jean shorts and an overlong orange T-shirt. He didn't want to frighten it.

"You miss your way?" he said when the child was close enough to hear him. "Go home."

The child paused dand stared at him surprised. For a moment he wondered if it didn't speak English. That wouldn't have surprised him much, there were many international travelers who came there. But, for some reason, he sensed the child understood English well. "Home," he repeated.

"I will."

"Where is your muda?"

The child shrugged.

"Hungry?"

The child shrugged again.

He sighed and stubbed out his cigarette, putting it in the tiny canister he'd brought with him. Discarded cigarette butts were a grounds for immediate dismissal. The owners took the image of the resort very seriously. Once the evidence of his vice was out of sight, he pulled out a piece of grater cake, which he liked to munch on before he went to work.

He saw the hunger in the child's eyes as it stared at the sweet coconut treat with its bright pink topping, which he held in his hand. He handed it over. The child carefully broke off a piece and then tucked the rest in the pocket of their worn shorts. He was surprised by the child's actions. He had expected it to shove the piece of grater cake in its mouth the way his own son liked to. And if the child was truly hungry it was too cautious.

The child wasn't an island one, the accent, from a mere two words, said US, but he'd have to listen more to be certain. But what were they doing here by themself? It was rare for tourists to have their kids wandering alone, especially looking like this. There was a story here. "Go alang home, you have no business here."

"Thank you," the child said in a soft voice before it headed back down along the beach.

He wouldn't think about it. The child wasn't his problem. Whoever was supposed to look after it was the one responsible. He turned away from the small silhouette as it became a tiny dot in the distance. He had to go over the orders for the VIP customers, the banquet and the final day of a convention that had kept the kitchen extra busy.

But in spite of his busy day, Charlie thought about the child that night. He didn't mean to and frankly didn't want to, but it kept coming back into his mind. Maybe because the child reminded him a bit of his sister. The lost look in its brown eyes. His sister, Mia, had that look before the day she decided to stand on a bridge and dive head first into a concrete river. It had been only three years after their father had abandoned the family, leaving his mother to take care of him and his two sisters. He'd been twelve; she fifteen.

His aunt had come to the rescue. She owned a restaurant and quickly gave his sisters and him work. Mia had hated it, but he hadn't. He'd worked in a kitchen since then. To him food meant family, fortune and freedom.

His aunt had been disappointed when he told her he didn't want to take over the restaurant, but he had different ambitions. He focused on winning local and regional baking competitions, which took him to New York where he trained as an apprentice at Le Fleur in Connecticut. He rose to assistant pastry chef before coming to the Star Moon where he'd worked for the past eight years. Food consumed his life. One day he hoped to live in America and open up a fudge shop. Usually he was always thinking about work, he didn't like thinking about his past or this strange child.

"What's troubling you?" his wife asked him that evening after dinner. She'd been telling him about a prodigy, some nine year old black boy who could play Chopin like a master, from the US she'd seen perform, but he'd barely listened.

"I'm fine," he said. He loved her but didn't like to confide in her. He didn't like to confide in anyone. He was a man used to keeping his thoughts to himself. Whatever troubled him was a burden he'd carry alone.

He wasn't surprised to see the child the next day and this time noticed it was a girl; if he were honest he'd admit that he was a little glad. If he saw the child then it was alive, nothing bad had happened to it. But that meant he'd have to deal with his uneasiness.

But he didn't want to. He was ending his shift when he saw Irene Patel, the front desk supervisor, shooing the child away from one of the outside tables, and realized he couldn't ignore the child any longer. "It's no trouble. She's with me."

"This thing?" Irene motioned to the child in disdain. She was a tall, slender Indian-Jamaican with dark lashes and hair who acted as if she were working at a palace. She hadn't taken any time to give him any notice, a lowly kitchen worker, she'd never once called him by name until the day she discovered where he'd obtained his certificate. Then her reverence for him increased. She'd confused his apprenticeship in Connecticut with a famed culinary school. He didn't tell her that he hadn't graduated from the Le Fleur she was thinking of but a technical school, he didn't feel the need to dissuade her since the misunderstanding worked in his favor.

"Yes, thank you. I know you have a lot of work to do."

She always said she did, although she usually gave her subordinates most of the duties.

"Never mind then." She pursed her lips before she walked away.

The child kept her head down.

He held out another piece of grater cake, he'd bought an extra one in case he'd see her again. She took it.

"Do you not have a home?" he asked.

It took her a moment before she said, "I have one."

"Then why aren't you in it?" In the light of the day and with the baseball cap gone he could see the girl's thick black hair pulled back in a ponytail, thick dark eye brows and angular chin. For some reason the tension in him increased. A little girl shouldn't be roaming around alone. It was dangerous.

She shrugged.

"My name is—" He briefly paused. He really hated giving his full name, but didn't have the conviction to change it. He sighed and started again. "My name is Charlie Chin. You can call me Mr. Charlie or CC. Nobody calls me Charles unless they want to swallow their teeth along with their tongue. What dey call you?"

"Rina, Mr. CC."

He shook his head. "No. It's either Mr. Charlie or CC."

She blinked.

He sighed. "Never mind."

"I'm strong and I can work."

She looked as strong as guava jelly; skinny with long limbs. "That might be, but I don't need your help."

When he saw her face fall he sighed. "But

perhaps...tomorrow come early. Meet me under the same palm tree. Understood?"

She smiled and nodded before she ran away. He didn't know what he'd do with her, but he'd find something. She'd likely get bored and never come back. That's what he'd hoped.

She was so small that people barely noticed her when he took her with him into the kitchen. He loved the heat, the energy, the movements. He felt the most alive with sweat streaming down his back, his arms aching. He placed her in the corner near the sink.

Once the day began he forgot about her amongst the whirl of the industrial-sized machines blending and mixing, the special orders, the prep, checking ingredients (one had been running low), scolding an intern who'd rushed through a batch of their signature ginger cookies.

In the kitchen he was no ordinary man. He was part of an army. He kept his unit in line, they delivered. It was brutal work, not for the faint of heart, just the way he liked it.

It was near the end of one shift that he noticed the child watching him. Not with fear, but awe. An awe he understood, he had caught the same bug as a child. It was like falling in love. A world that had once seemed grey, suddenly burst into color. He saw the untapped passion and silent questions shining in her eyes, and knew it was real. Most people saw the end product as a cake or cookie and thought that being a pastry chef was an easy sweet profession. But she saw the dirty side, the hard work and loved it. She made him feel ten feet tall. He couldn't stop a smile.

In that one moment they looked at each other and bonded. Bonded over a love that needed no words. Food had saved his life. It could save hers too.

The kitchen was no place for a child, but she kept out of the way and just watched. He'd never been around a child who took up so little space. She didn't move. She stayed where he put her and when the kitchen was clear he taught her what he knew and she followed instructions with a serious intent. He gave her a little piece of dough to knead then showed her how to mold cookies.

In her he noticed something special. She took care, focused on details and precision, two skills important to a pastry chef. She was a natural. One who would one day do great things.

This love would take her far.

CHAPTER SEVEN

"Where have you been?"

"Nowhere," Rina told the cook as she closed the back door. She'd learned that lying was easy when no one cared what you had to say.

"It's late. Next time, mind the time you get home. You want me to get into trouble?" she said. She had hard eyes like Aunt Sonia, but her voice was never frosty.

"I won't."

"Did you pick up the shopping?"

She'd bought the items hours ago and had put them away in the fridge, not that anyone would have noticed. Or perhaps she just wanted to scold her, she'd grown used to that. "Yes."

"Give me a bottle then."

Ginger beer with hardo bread was the cook's favorite snack.

Rina didn't stay out late the next time, but also made sure not to get caught coming home. She had been pretending to be a ghost and it had worked, people looked right through her, nobody saw her and it was lonely, but Mr. CC had seen her and spoken to her.

And then he'd taken her into an amazing new world filled with sights and sounds she'd never seen or heard before. Everything moved so fast but beautiful things rose from the steel tables—layers of cakes, sheets of cookies and elaborate pastries, dough pounded and rolled and molded. And Mr. CC was a magician who others respected.

She loved spending time with him. He was a hard worker and kind. He taught her things about food she'd never known. Plus, he was respected and people paid attention to him. One day she wanted to wear a white jacket and work in a kitchen just like him.

Visiting with him then sneaking back into the house was easy. No one knew she was gone. Her grandparents were too busy visiting friends when they weren't worried about their son and the two women he kept busy with.

That first summer when Rina returned to the States and the house (she couldn't call it a home) in Maryland, she listened to their stories about their fabulous Hawaiian travels and looked over their pictures. They were kind enough to bring her back tiny souvenirs. A trinket here or there. She didn't have much to give them in return and that made her feel bad.

So the second summer she took pictures of the beach, never of the attractive but tiny house where her grandparents lived. She told them stories about drinking sweet coconut water straight from the source, the feel of the island breeze in the morning as she walked with the cook along the beach to the local market. The kindly pastor who always waved when they passed by his chapel. The scent of jerk chicken and spices.

She didn't talk about sneaking out in the morning to go to the Star Moon resort kitchen; about Mr. CC and the sweet scent of powdered sugar, the taste of freshly melted chocolate. She didn't tell them that her grandparents' cook took her to church every Sunday and they stayed there all day in the hot crowded one room until her skin started to itch.

She didn't tell them about their handsome Uncle and how he would have her lie to the women who showed up at the door looking for him. She didn't know why he ran away from them. They both seemed very nice. From her grandmother she'd learned one was a teacher at a girl's school and the other owned a shop that sold perfumes.

Rina didn't care that she was never in any of the pictures. Just that her cousins were impressed.

The year she turned ten, her Uncle got married to a wealthy woman from the city who wanted a man with good looks and no sense, her grandfather passed away after a fun night of dominoes, and her grandmother went to live with her younger sister in a house so small the two of them could barely occupy a room without touching, so there was barely room for a growing girl. Therefore she was sent to a kind second cousin who lived in the same neighborhood and slept most of the day and didn't care what Rina did as long as she was quiet, leaving Rina free to visit the resort without trouble.

The year she turned eleven, Mr. CC disappeared.

"He's gone," a coffee colored woman with pencil thin

brows told Rina when she went to see him at the kitchen entrance, eager to see what the next two months would bring. The woman blocked her path.

"Gone?"

"Him mother catch cancer. He take another position closer to where she lives so he can be with her."

She didn't get to say goodbye. She didn't get to thank him.

"Can I still come..." She let her words trail away as the woman shook her head. "CC was able to get away with a lot of things the rest of us can't. Go your ways and be happy. He'd want that. We all do. Oh, before I forget." She disappeared to the back then returned with a thick envelope. "He wanted you to have this."

Rina held back tears and managed a nod before she turned and walked away.

She walked to the beach and sat under the same palm tree where she'd first spotted Mr. CC smoking. She'd never expected him to call out to her; most adults pretended she wasn't there. But he'd seen her.

Rina blinked back tears as she opened the envelope. There was no note or letter inside, just sheets of paper stapled together with a series of recipes written in his bold hand.

Rina stared at it in awe. It was the greatest gift anyone had ever given her. She held the sheets of recipes close to her chest and cried.

She cried because she loved him and she'd miss him.

She cried because she'd never get to know if he'd achieve his dream of traveling to America and opening a fudge shop.

She cried because she'd never see him again.

And she cried because he'd made her feel important. In that moment she faced her destiny and knew she wanted to make him proud. She would study and practice every chance she got.

She used that chance the following summer when Rina had to spend it with her mother and father and siblings. She copied some of Mr. CC's recipes; she left the originals in a safe box underneath her bed, and used them to bake cookies and brownies which she sold for extra money. Her parents were impressed by her entrepreneurial spirit and quickly grew dependent on the money she brought in.

She learned to keep some of the money hidden so that it could last when her father decided to host his friends and stock up on lottery tickets and liquor, rather than restock the kitchen with necessary items like food.

Everything changed when she turned fifteen. She decided to do an apprenticeship. If she wanted to be like Mr. CC she had to start early and home economic courses wouldn't be enough. She had thought of dropping out of high school and devoting all her time to her dream, but Uncle Timothy forbade it. And apprenticeship was the next best thing. She was on her own. As kind as the Parkers were to her, she knew she couldn't depend on them.

Every summer they traveled without her and she knew she could only depend on herself.

But for some reason Amelia wanted to do an apprenticeship too, imagining a heavenly summer filled with sweets, then Carla said she wanted to stop her dance lessons, which annoyed Aunt Sonia who felt that Rina's action had influenced Carla. The bickering and whining irritated Uncle Timothy so much that he decided it was time Rina traveled with them as a family and that put an end to her plans and everyone else's.

Because of the stories and pictures Rina had shared with them, her cousins were eager for a trip to the Caribbean so her apprenticeship was abandoned, for a while, and for the first time since she'd move to the house in Brandon she got to travel with the Parker family.

Rina couldn't believe her good fortune.

A trip to Barbados. She didn't care that she spent most of the time applying sunscreen on Aunt Lauren's back or running errands for Aunt Sonia, she was away from the cramped apartment in Virginia and her mother's ever growing dissatisfaction. Her mother didn't laugh the way she used to and while there were no more jokes about disappearing feet, there was little laughter in the house at all.

She felt a little guilty for not wanting to be with her, but hoped to be a success one day so she could help her parents and her brothers and sisters.

The resort where they stayed reminded Rina of the one in Jamaica, but she had no one to tell that to. No one to tell about the friendly man who'd let her help him in the kitchen. Someone she may never see again. She stood on the beach, letting the water wash over her feet.

She felt small staring out at the vast ocean, but not as small as when she was in school. She wasn't the brightest student and she knew that disappointed her Uncle.

Her Aunt Sonia reminded her of how clever her mother had been that she must have gotten the worst of her father's family. But one day she'd show them that they hadn't made a mistake for letting her stay with them. She'd become somebody they could be proud of. She thought of the notes and recipes Mr. CC had given her. She would use them and one day become someone great who people would finally notice.

"DO YOU THINK WE NEED TO WORRY ABOUT HER?" Sonia said as she watched Rina from the hotel window.

"Worry about what?" Lauren said with a tired sigh. She really didn't want to have to worry about anything.

"She's well past the age when she should be thinking of boys."

"Rina's not ready yet."

"She could make a mistake like her mother. Find a no good man and ruin her life."

"That's a ways away. I think she will be fine."

"It's important to watch her and not allow her too much freedom. I think that's where our parents went wrong with poor Isabel. She was headstrong and didn't have a firm parental hand to guide her."

"I don't think Rina will be any trouble, she hasn't been so far."

No, but Sonia saw a child full of secrets. These past several years, as Sonia watched Rina grow, she became even more distrustful of her. The girl was too serene, too obliging. Even her parents had said there was no sign of temper, no disobedience, nothing to complain about. The child wasn't normal.

All those stories and photos from her time in Jamaica were too studied. There were never pictures of people in the photos. Only one or two of her grandparents, but then the rest were of strangers in the market, on the beach, walking along the road.

The girl had instilled envy in her cousins. Her cousins who had traveled farther, they'd been taught French and Latin since the age of three, seen the Louvre and the pyramids in Egypt, dined with dignitaries and had more adventures than most, yet the girl who would have been a high school drop out if Timothy hadn't interfered, whose grades were unremarkable, she'd managed to poison their hearts.

No, Sonia would continue to watch her. She sensed the child had a special destiny.

A destiny tied to them all.

PART II

"Make the most of yourself by fanning the tiny, inner sparks of possibility into flames of achievement."

Golda Meir

CHAPTER EIGHT

He wasn't coming.

Rina realized there was a strange moment of quiet doom when one realizes they've been stood up. That moment happened to her as she stood outside a DC theater waiting for her date to arrive.

Only two minutes before she hadn't felt that way.

Two minutes before she still couldn't believe he'd said yes.

She'd checked her reflection in her pocket mirror one more time, adjusting the peach scarf Amelia had given her years ago, and took a deep breath. Tonight was really happening, she had a date with Brian Dixon. He was the son of the restaurant owner where she worked as a pastry chef. He was very easy to talk to and although handsome he didn't flaunt it. She was surprised he was still single. But perhaps his schedule was too busy to meet anyone. Lucky her.

It had taken all her courage to ask him out. She'd

bought theater tickets after overhearing him say he liked going to the theater.

He reminded her of Mr. CC. He had a warm grin and a passion for food. He was always careful in the kitchen and she enjoyed working with him. Now she'd get a chance to know him even more.

Then the fissures of uncertainty began to gather as soft as the gentle evening settling over the city, a brush of a spring wind toying with the hem of her dress. The sense that something was wrong.

She waited in front of the theater, first ten then fifteen minutes before she called him and was sent straight to voicemail. A half hour later she knew he wasn't coming.

At the bakery that Monday she saw him walk into the kitchen brown-skinned and broad-shouldered with an easy smile for one of the workers and tried to read him. He looked right past her. She didn't know what to make of it. Had she gone into ghost mode by accident?

At twenty-five she felt she was living her dream. This restaurant was her third position. After high school, she'd landed an entry-level position at a local bakery before serving as a pastry cook and chocolatier at a Las Vegas hotel. But she'd quickly gotten restless and decided to take a Spanish Patisserie class at the French Pastry School before landing her current job in the cozy Maryland restaurant.

She went into ghost mode, making herself as quiet and still as possible, as she had done many times so that people wouldn't notice her, but she'd never done it with him. He was one of the few people who actually spoke to her. Hadn't he said he'd meet her? If he'd changed his mind why hadn't he told her? Why was he suddenly acting so distant? She didn't have much time before she had to return to her station and prepare for the day. She had to do something.

She went up to him. "Ummm...what happened?"

He blinked. "What do you mean?"

"We had a date."

"We did?"

She stumbled over her words. "I bought theater tickets, remember? You said you'd go with me."

He shrugged. "Sorry, must have skipped my mind." He patted her on the arm before he turned and walked away.

Had she misread him? Had it all been a dream? Maybe she hadn't really asked him out. She'd daydreamed about it enough times, perhaps it hadn't been real. The thought made her heart sink. But he seemed genuinely perplexed and she didn't think he was the type of person to stand someone up. Maybe she'd try again another time.

But later that day she overheard something that made his intentions clear.

"I felt put on the spot," Rina overheard him say as she was getting strawberries from storage. "That's the only reason I said yes. I know that was a mistake."

"But she likes you," she recognized the voice as the assistant chef.

He laughed. "Who doesn't?"

"Don't be mean."

"If she weren't so good at what she does, I would have turned her down flat. She creeps me out."

"I like her. She's nice."

"Have you looked at her?"

The assistant coughed, or laughed, Rina wasn't sure. "Be nice."

"I know I should. She covers for me enough times I'm grateful and she makes Mom happy."

Rina felt ill.

Brian thought she was creepy? He'd only said yes to please his mother? How could she have read him so wrong? He was like Aunt Sonia—someone who she'd tried to make love her but never could. She had learned her lesson. She was only useful, never lovable.

For all his smiles she knew Uncle Timothy liked her but didn't love her, neither did Aunt Lauren. Her parents loved the money she could send them. Her cousins, Carla and Amelia, liked her when she was useful, but forgot her when she was not. And now Brian.

Brian had fooled her. She wouldn't be fooled again.

It was at that moment she built a mask of iron, one to cover her face and one to cover her heart. She would never risk it again, she'd give all her passion to her work. No one would ever pierce through her defenses and hurt her like this again.

BARBARA DIXON FOUND THE YOUNG WOMAN WHO SAT in front of her a little terrifying. There was something different about her, a little ruthless, almost fierce.

Barbara had only known Rina Powell for eighteen months, but it was her ingenuity and skill that had turned her failing business around.

However, what Rina had told her, made Barbara's heart grow cold. "What do you mean you want to quit? Why all of a sudden? I thought you were happy here."

Rina looked at her and blinked.

"Tell me what you want and we can—"

"I can't stay. I'm sorry," Rina said but she didn't sound sorry at all. She sounded angry and bitter. Barbara knew she had no choice but to let her go.

And Rina left that day eager to get as far away from Brian, the bakery and her foolish romantic dreams as possible.

She didn't look for another position right away. She gave herself a week to process what she'd done and needed time to think of what she'd do next. She had enough money for the rent of her small apartment and she didn't have many bills to worry about.

She kept to a routine. She woke up early as usual, tried one of Mr. CC's recipes, studied a new baking technique, watched a cooking show, read a little before heading to bed.

She also ran every day, even in the rain. A warm rain that helped to hide her tears. That made her feel clean when most of her life she'd been made to feel dirty, unwanted, repellent.

It was on one of those lonely, rain soaked runs that she had a heart attack.

It was only through luck that Keith Marlow saw the woman vomit then collapse. He'd been driving through the tree lined neighborhood, returning home after picking his son and daughter up from karate. He rarely paid attention to joggers. There were so many healthy freaks in the neighborhood from bicyclists, walkers, runners. Hell, even his wife was starting to nag him that an evening stroll was something they should start doing together.

No, he wouldn't have paid any attention to the jogger if she hadn't been weaving. She also looked distressed. It was only by chance when he was looking back at his son to warn him to stop kicking his sister's chair that in the rearview mirror he saw the woman lying motionless on the ground.

He quickly pulled to the side of the road and raced over to her.

He halted at the sight. She was so small and thin. If he hadn't seen that she'd been upright only a few seconds ago, he'd have thought he'd happened on a corpse. In her sleek black windbreaker she looked like a dead bird washed up in the rain. He didn't know what came over him to take off his coat and wrap it around her. He called the ambulance.

"Is she breathing?" the operator asked.

His heart pounded so much he could hardly hear his reply. "I don't know."

"Can you feel a pulse?"

"I don't know," he said again and he hated saying the words even though they were true. He didn't know anything!! He knew panicking wouldn't help her, but he couldn't focus. She didn't seem to be breathing and if there was a pulse it was too faint to be felt and he didn't want to think she was dead. That he'd watched someone drop dead in his rearview mirror. Didn't it take a couple of minutes to die?

"Sir," the operator said in a calm, but firm voice. "I will need you to do some chest compressions."

"What?"

"Chest compressions."

"I don't know how to do that." He'd taken CPR classes when his son was born and forgotten everything. Besides, a grown woman was vastly different than an infant.

"Sir, you will be fine. Put the phone on speaker. I will walk you through it."

As he pressed on her chest and followed the instructions he hoped she would open her eyes. He hoped she would gasp for breath or something, but the only way her body moved was through him.

His voice cracked with desperation. "It's not working."

"You're doing great, the ambulance is almost there. This is important, don't stop."

He didn't but the ambulance seemed to take forever, then he heard the wail of the siren.

Minutes later he saw her being carted off. He wanted to follow them, but he needed to get his kids home.

He needed them to be safe. He didn't want to know that he'd failed. He wasn't sure he'd done much. He was a simple man. He wanted to be a hero, but seeing that woman he felt defeated that anyone could save her.

CHAPTER NINE

*S*omething was wrong.

Rina looked up at her Aunt Lauren's worried face and then Aunt Sonia's annoyed one.

"What's going on?" she asked. She turned to her left and noticed the white walls and medical equipment standing by her bed and the tube attached to her arm.

"You had a fainting spell," Aunt Lauren said.

"It was a bloody heart attack," Aunt Sonia said in a sharp tone. "At your age. Can you imagine? What are you doing to yourself?"

"A heart attack?" Rina said. How could that make any sense?

Aunt Lauren pinched the bridge of her nose as if pained. "Tact, Sonia. Try to have a little tact. She's unwell."

"Anyone can see that. It's just a show for attention."

Rina closed her eyes. She didn't want to be here, she wanted to be away. She had been running. That's the last thing she remembered: Running. Feeling sick. After that…nothing…

She kept her eyes closed. "How did I get here?"

"A man with his kids found you," Aunt Lauren said. "They don't know who he is."

Aunt Sonia sniffed. "You're lucky."

"You have to take better care of yourself."

She opened her eyes. "I take good care." She'd been taking care of herself for years; she didn't ask anything from them.

Aunt Sonia folded her arms. "If that were the case you wouldn't be here."

Aunt Lauren lightly touched Rina's arm. "What is wrong, dear?"

"Nothing." Rina didn't know why Aunt Lauren was looking at her that way. It had been nearly three years since she'd last seen them. She'd always managed to be too busy to visit during the holidays. Even as a child Aunt Lauren never used to fuss over her before.

"When can I go home?" She had so much she needed to do, like find another job. But she couldn't tell them that.

"You need to be here another day for tests and then we'll see where you can stay."

"I have a place to stay."

"Darling, this is serious," Aunt Lauren said. "You nearly died. You can't keep this up."

"Keep what up?"

Aunt Sonia's mouth became hard. "If you want to pretend you don't know—"

Aunt Lauren touched her sister's shoulder. "Sonia, that's enough."

Aunt Sonia closed her mouth, but she didn't move. She stared at Rina with unchecked anger in her gaze. "Vanity is a sin," she said in an acid tone before she turned and left.

"We are family and we are here for you," Aunt Lauren said. "There's no need for you to do this kind of behavior to get our attention."

Rina furrowed her brows confused. "I don't know what you're talking about."

She patted her hand. "That's fine. Just rest."

She couldn't understand why they thought something was wrong.

Nobody from her family knew about her feelings about Brian. She rarely spoke to them much anymore except to hear how well Carla was doing in her studies or what new project Amelia was up to.

THERE WERE TESTS AND TALKS OF FEEDING TUBES and questions and Rina answered them all the best she could. Lying wasn't as easy because her replies seemed to matter.

Her uncle and cousins had visited her the other day and it hadn't gone well.

Uncle Timothy looked grim. Amelia had taken one look at her and burst into tears. But she could be so dramatic sometimes. Carla stared at her in shock, but neither had been in a hospital before. That was probably what was upsetting them. The bed, machines, tube and such.

She smiled.

They didn't smile back.

She didn't understand why they were all being so serious.

The medical staff told her that she had to take care, that if she didn't take care of herself she could face brittle bones and possible organ failure. But she *did* take care of herself, she always had. Plus she was young and before this she'd been healthy. She didn't see why they were so concerned. All she knew was that she wanted to get away so she could leave the hospital and rebuild her life.

She was thinking of the best way to convince everyone she was okay when a big, bright orange rolled into her room.

CHAPTER TEN

The orange rolled over the white tile and hit the foot of her bed. Rina stared down at it then heard movement and saw a man wearing a grey robe standing in her doorway. He looked to be in his early to mid twenties. For a moment her breath caught and she feared she was having another attack. He was that striking, that physically beautiful. Not in a classical sense, there were no fine features and delicate curves. He was too rugged for that, his jaw line a little too sharp, his shoulders a little too broad, but he had a face she could study for hours.

Like chocolate fondant cast over the body of a man.

"Um...I'm sorry," he said and she realized his voice fit his face perfectly, just the right tenor with a deep husky undertone that made her pulse quicken. She'd never reacted to another person, let alone a man, like this before and she wondered what medications the hospital had been giving her.

"It's okay," she said when she saw the man hesitate. "You can come in."

"Thank you." He gingerly walked over to the bed and tried to reach for the orange then winced in pain and jerked back.

"Wait, let me get it." Rina swung her legs over the side of the bed, feeling a little winded when she did so, but then managed to grab the orange and hand it to him. He held out his hand and forced a smile, but she noticed he looked a little pale and worried that he'd end up dropping it again.

"You should sit down."

To her relief he didn't argue and sat in a chair near her bed. He briefly closed his eyes and took a deep breath. He looked exhausted. "Thanks."

She began to place the orange in his lap then hesitated when she noticed that some of the rind had been peeled away. "Want me to finish peeling it for you?"

His eyes remained closed, but she saw his shoulders relax. "That would be wonderful."

He was so silent as she peeled the orange that she wondered if he'd fallen asleep. But when she finally managed to finish, she looked up at him and saw him watching her.

He not only had a handsome face he had nice eyes. But she wouldn't fall for that again. She didn't know anyone. She didn't know how they really thought or felt about things. She wouldn't be lied to again.

"Here," she said.

"Take half."

"But—"

He shook his head. "Don't argue, just take it. The rest will go to waste."

She bit into the juicy fruit, feeling oddly warmed by the gesture.

He continued to study her in a manner that was both unnerving and flattering at the same time. He didn't make her feel like a ghost. "What brings you here?" he finally said.

"Heart attack they tell me."

He nodded. "Stab wound."

"Ouch."

He nodded again. "I didn't move fast enough this time."

"This time? You've had knives come at you before?"

A faint smile touched his lips and lightened his brown eyes. "Who said it was a knife?"

"It wasn't?"

He shook his head.

"What was it?"

His smile widened. "Scissors."

She didn't know why he found that amusing. She didn't find it very funny at all.

"They tell me I'll live."

"That's good."

"And you?"

"They think something's wrong with me."

"Your heart?"

"No, just me. They think I'm too skinny or something."

He nodded, but she saw no judgment in his eyes, just a quiet acceptance. He was easy to talk to. He may be pretending to be nice to her, she didn't care. She wanted someone to pretend that she really mattered. But she didn't want to reveal too much to this stranger. Like Mr. CC he'd disappear. She forced a yawn. "I'm really tired."

He carefully stood to his feet. "Sorry again."

"Glad I could help. Be careful of sharp objects."

He chuckled then winced. "I will. And you take care of that heart of yours," he said with an intensity that made her entire body grow warm. Why did his words shake her? Why did she want to say she would? Instead she bit her lip, nodded and watched him walk out the door, wishing he could stay a little longer.

CHAPTER ELEVEN

*I*f you'd listened to me, this wouldn't have happened.

Warren Ross sighed as he slowly made his way back to his hospital room. His mother had barely given him any time since he'd arrived there. He'd been lucky she'd been called away because of some issue at the music school she owned, so that he could get some space from her. But he knew she'd be back soon. Too soon. No matter how honeyed the words sounded in her Jamaican lilt her words soured his soul.

He walked into his hospital room and softly swore when he saw the back of the man standing there. Before he could sneak back out the man turned and faced him.

"What happened?" his older brother said.

"I went for a walk and dropped my orange and it rolled—"

His brother frowned. "What are you talking about?"

"I thought you asked me what happened."

Peter shook his head. "I mean the other night. And why aren't you in bed?"

"Walking is good." Warren took off his robe and got back in the bed.

"So are you going to tell me?"

Warren looked at his brother and shook his head. "Nothing happened."

"'Nothing' doesn't get you put in the hospital with stitches."

"A misunderstanding."

"Another misunderstanding like that can get you killed."

"It's nothing."

His voice became urgent. "Listen, you've got to let me help you. I don't—"

"You're here. You've got a family. I don't need you looking after me anymore."

"Mom thinks—"

He shot his brother a look. "Don't mention her."

He sighed. "If you'll just—"

"I'm not going back."

"Nobody says you have to go back. I, for one, understand—"

"No, you don't. You don't understand what it was like to have no identity. No peace. I wasn't allowed to have a thought of my own without permission. I'm not doing that again. You weren't treated the same. You were able to make a life. I'm claiming that chance now."

His brother hung his head, ashamed. "I know. You're right."

"I'm fine really."

He fell silent a moment, folded his arms before he lifted his head and said, "How long are you going to lie to yourself?"

Warren narrowed his eyes, his voice hard. "I'm not lying. It's my life."

"And you could lose it."

"I won't."

His brother shook his head. "You don't know that."

"Neither do you." His brother always thought he could predict things; it had served him well in business. He knew when to pull out of a business deal and when to stay put. He had an eight year advantage on Warren and felt he knew all the ways of the world, but Warren knew that in life there was a lot of grey.

He wasn't a child prodigy anymore. A time when everything was planned—his destiny set. Now he was a man fighting for his freedom.

Now things were more complicated. He wanted what his brother had, a sense of normalcy, but it still remained out of reach. One day he'd claim it. He wouldn't stop until he did.

His family didn't understand why he'd made the choices he had, but he didn't need them to. He would stick with the life he'd chosen to lead. He wouldn't waver. That wasn't the kind of man he was. And he didn't want his brother treating him like a child.

Although, at one moment, when the scissors had pierced his flesh, he briefly thought of curling into a ball and letting it happen, not defending himself, the pain felt good, it felt natural, almost healing. A part of him felt that he deserved it. That he was exactly where he was supposed to be.

He couldn't get his brother to understand. But one day he would.

It was his life.

A life he'd never had before. He'd never had the choice. He'd fight for his freedom no matter what it cost him. His gaze drifted to the bouquet of flowers and large orange balloon, which reminded him of the young black woman in the other room.

She looked so frail, but her voice was melodic and soothing, even her gaze. One would have thought it would look haunted to match the rest of her thin frame, but there was warmth there, kindness. True kindness. She didn't have to let him stay in her room and peel an orange for him, make him feel less alone, yet she had. He almost wanted to tell her about the reason he was still in the hospital, that the scissor attack had brought him here, but it was an infection that had nearly killed him that had kept him there. But that was over. He almost wanted to tell her how beautiful she was both inside and out.

"Mom—"

Warren shifted his gaze and looked at his brother. "You can leave now," he said. Even lying in his bed with a stab wound in his side Warren knew he was stronger than his brother. His will was greater. He would not bend.

Peter knew it too and lowered his gaze defeated. He sighed, patted Warren's hand before he turned and left.

Warren returned his gaze to the large bouquet of flowers from his wife. She'd wept when he'd finally recovered and he'd held her hand and told her it was okay. That he would be fine.

And he would be.

That's what his brother didn't understand. That no matter what happened, in the end he always was.

CHAPTER TWELVE

He came back.

Rina blinked twice to make sure she wasn't dreaming.

She wasn't dreaming about a beautiful man dressed in blue jeans and a green polo T-shirt standing beside her bed holding out a yellow rose to her.

She stared at it, almost afraid to touch it. Almost afraid to move.

"You don't want it?" he said and his voice pulled her out of her paralysis.

"What is this?" she managed to say, even though that wasn't what she'd meant to say. She'd meant to ask him why he was there, why he was giving her something, anything.

He placed the rose on her lap. "I have so many I thought you could use one," he said. He was kind enough not to look around her room and make her aware of the lack of flowers or gifts anywhere. Just one lonely greeting card.

"But—"

"Just take it. It will lose its scent and die anyway, there's no need for it to go to waste."

"Thank you," she said. It was a shame she hated roses, but he didn't need to know that. She struggled to sit up straighter and adjust the pillows behind her.

"May I?" he said before he reached behind her and adjusted the pillows.

She lifted the rose and sniffed it just to give herself something to do. Soon she was reminded of the sweet taste of cherries in July and the warm sensation of sand between her toes. But it wasn't the scent of the flower that did it. It was the scent of him. His scent took her away from the hospital bed, from her feelings of loneliness, just as the scents in the bakery had.

Anytime she felt alone she would bake bread and sit with her eyes closed and inhale the scent and be whisked back to her past. When, for a brief moment, she'd sort of belonged; when she'd had a friend and mentor who was there for her.

"I'm leaving today," he said.

Rina blinked. It took her a moment to realize he'd stepped away from her; that she was holding the stem of the flower so tight it could break.

It hurt to hear his words, but it was nice to have a chance to say goodbye.

"I...uh..." Her words fell away. She had so much she wanted to say but didn't know how.

He rubbed his forehead. "You—"

"There you are," a woman said, coming into the room. She hurried over to him and looped her arm through his. When he patted her hand in reassurance, Rina noticed the ring on his finger. The wedding ring.

The big, gold band shining against his brown skin.

The big warning sign that he was taken and off-limits.

Somehow she hadn't seen it before or hadn't wanted to.

They made a beautiful couple. The woman by his side with her pretty, gentle face and light brown hair had a slender build and dainty hands. She appeared to be in her early to mid thirties and looked very attentive and worried. She hovered over him and he seemed to take pleasure in that. Rina wondered how it must feel to have someone fuss over her like that. She also wondered who would have wanted to stab him with a pair of scissors.

"We should go and leave her to rest," his wife said.

"No, it's okay," Rina said, but she could tell the woman wasn't listening as she tried to tug him towards the door. Rina couldn't understand her eagerness to leave. It wasn't as if Rina was any competition.

However, his wife's efforts failed. He didn't move. Instead he wrapped his hand around Rina's wrist, and said with feeling in his voice, "Take care of yourself."

His hands were as beautiful as the rest of him. Strong, but gentle. Whether it was the warmth of his grip or the tenderness of his gaze, something made her briefly cover his hand with hers. She covered his hand not wanting to let go. She wanted to feel his hand, his skin, beneath hers. Make a connection.

She wanted to keep him there a little while longer,

she wanted to gain courage, she wanted to know more about him. She wanted to know how such a beautiful man could look both happy and sad at the same time. She wanted to understand the feelings he ignited within her. But she knew she couldn't.

She quickly, and with a little shame, pulled her hand away before he could and said in a quiet voice, "You too."

He smiled before he finally let his wife pull him out the door.

Rina waited a few seconds before she followed them.

She didn't know why, but once they left her room she followed them into the corridor and stopped just shy of the elevators.

She followed them because she wanted to imprint him in her memory. She wanted to listen for his name since she hadn't gotten the chance to ask. She wanted to briefly be a part of their world. A world filled with love and care. The woman by his side seemed to care for him very much and Rina could tell that he loved her. And Rina's heart ached because...because she wondered what it would be like to be loved by someone like him. But no matter how much it hurt she couldn't look away.

His smile was soft when his wife asked him a question and he nodded in reply. Rina wondered how they'd met, how long they'd been married. Neither her father nor uncle ever looked at their wives like that. So tenderly, with such understanding, as if he wanted to reassure her even more than was necessary.

If he were hers, she wouldn't need that. Just a gaze or a smile would be enough. But she was happy for him. A kind man deserved a kind woman. That wasn't always the case.

Her mother rarely laughed anymore and neither did her father. Few of his friends came to visit anymore. Death in one form or another had whittled their numbers. His temper flared more quickly than in the past. Rina sent money when she could. Her mother was always grateful, although she hinted it wasn't really enough. One day Rina planned to make sure it would be. One day she'd get a big place and take care of them.

That was the only kind of love she knew.

"Are you sure you're okay? Maybe you need more time."

"I'm fine truly." Warren walked with his wife towards the hospital exit. He loved her most when she was like this. When she took care of him, cared about him. This was the reason that others didn't understand. The reason why he stayed. Why he was determined to make his marriage work.

She drove him home and made him one of his favorite meals: cheese stuffed grilled peppers and penne with asparagus. He ate it and felt warmth run through him. It was good to be out of the hospital. Good to be away from the doctors, nurses and endless questions. This was peace. Dodging suspicions, dodging judgment. He wouldn't let his life be judged, his choices questioned. His entire life had been about control, he was taking that control back. He wasn't a child anymore, he wasn't a puppet on display. He had cut the strings.

His wife cut up fruit for him and he stared at the orange slices and thought about *her* again.

Her...the woman who seemed to be hungry for something else other than food.

He hoped she found it before it was too late.

He hoped she understood the meaning of his words.

He took a bite of the sweet fruit and remembered the whisper-like sensation of the woman's hand covering his.

He swallowed the fruit and thought of her and belatedly wished he knew her name.

CHAPTER THIRTEEN

It had become like a game.

At twenty-seven, she knew the benefits of planning and she knew how to plan well.

Today she planned carefully, looked at all the angles. She knew almost every corner of the building, its blind spots. Her goal was to get inside and not get caught. So far she'd managed it twice. She was going for a triple.

Rina put her sports bag over her shoulder and walked into the gym. She made sure to wear loose fitting clothes and dark glasses. The person at the front desk was new and had never see her before, didn't know her history, that was a plus. She would make that work in her favor.

She made it to the lockers without detection.

Success!

This was the farthest she'd come in a while. But would she make it to the machines? Did she want to? She'd come this far, that was a win. But if one of the regulars spotted her...? She took a deep breath. It was worth the risk.

She was better now. Her heart was good. She had a right to be here. It had been two years since her heart attack, she deserved this.

She walked into the main area and got on the tread-mill, she'd only managed a few steps before they came for her.

"You know you're not supposed to be here," one of the trainers, a toned woman in yoga pants and a T-Shirt said.

Rina kept walking.

"I know you can hear me."

Rina sighed and turned off the machine.

"You made a promise," she said.

"I was forced to."

"For your own good. Do you think it was easy—"

"It's okay, I'm leaving." She didn't want to hear the guilt in the woman's voice. She'd once thought of her as a friend. But friends don't get friends locked away. And that was what had happened to her. She'd survived her heart attack, gotten better with the help of some coun-selors she didn't think she needed, gotten another job and joined a gym hoping to make friends. Instead, within three months they'd rejected her, called authorities and got her locked up.

Not that where she'd been sent was a prison.

No, a prison wasn't something ones family had to pay for. Aunt Sonia reminded her how much she was costing them. No, it wasn't a prison. The converted mansion was called an inpatient rehab facility for people with eating disorders. It only felt like that. A place of group meetings, scheduled weigh-ins, scheduled meals and doors that had to be kept open.

It was her second time, since the hospital, she'd been in a place to help her deal with a problem that she had under control. Sure, after her heart attack, she'd been in denial, but now she wasn't. She had to be careful, she knew that. She could die. She knew that too.

She exercised because it made her feel good, it was a good life choice. She didn't do it to manage her weight. Going to the gym made her feel less alone. Sure she could work out by herself, there was no one else to stop her, but the gym had felt like a community of like-minded people. But they'd kicked her out. Said she wasn't one of them.

She'd been barred from the gym only eight months ago, but it felt like a lifetime.

"We don't want to have to call the police. But I will."

It was an empty threat, but Rina had gotten used to people saying what they didn't really mean.

She thought about her defeat the next day while working at the Bee Sweet bakery as she checked the freezer and noticed all the biscuits had been eaten, pretzels too. She'd also checked to make sure they had enough chocolate sauce and financiers, a small French almond cake. Plus they were known for their nut-free cupcakes so she'd have to prepare for a rush on them.

Tuesdays were busy, but she loved it that way. Here she was home. This bakery had saved her.

It had given her purpose.

Here life made sense. You put dough in a bowl to rise, you wash your hands, you make fondue, you wash your hands, you get the bread baskets and pie pans ready. You think about brulees, inhale the scent of cinnamon rolls, whip cream, make a custard base.

Rina loved it all. She put her every thought and emotion into each action. She knew that timing was everything in baking so she became even more particular about every minute, every second—like Mr. CC had done. She'd learned to not fight time, but harness it so that every dessert could be a tiny masterpiece.

Every day she set out to make the patrons never forget her, they may forget her face or name, most would never know who she was, but once their tongues touched a soft cupcake, its moist layers melting on their tongue or the luxurious feel of a triple chocolate semifreddo (a type of semi-frozen dessert), she'd have planted herself in their subconscious forever.

She'd have them seeking out this sensation for the rest of their lives. Like a ghost, she'd haunt them.

And they'd come back for more.

But most of all, as she worked, every day she thought of him. The man who'd given her a flower, the one with kind eyes and a shy smile. She imagined baking for him. Giving him back the kindness he'd generously offered her. The thought of him still made her pulse race, but it made her feel alive instead of like a ghost. It also gave her meaning. Purpose.

During her break she checked her phone and saw three messages from Amelia. Her cousin was desperate to talk to her about something and Rina kept putting her off. Twice Amelia had wanted them to go into business together, Rina shuddered at the idea. While Amelia always had the backing of her father she wasn't the best with money.

She ignored her cousin's calls and messages and steadily worked through the day, but the moment her day started to come to a close and the manager called her into his office she sensed that the day wasn't going to end well.

CHAPTER FOURTEEN

Fired or dumped.

From the look on her boss's face, Julian was going to do one or the other. Since Rina was not dating him, she knew it had to be the former. Fired.

"Rina, you are a great worker..."

She inwardly sighed and looked over his trimmed goatee. She knew he got his hair trimmed every week and likely a facial that kept his smooth brown skin glistening. He sat in front of the large Bee Sweet logo (a smiling bumblebee and half eaten chocolate chip cookie) he'd had posted on the wall, his hands clasped together like he was posing for a camera. He was going to compliment her then fire her. That would take more time and energy to pretend that it didn't matter.

"And it wasn't an easy decision to make..."

Just get to the point. She knew that he was close to the baker and he and Rina didn't get on the greatest.

"Can I ask why?"

He blinked quickly. "I'm sorry?"

"Why am I getting fired?"

He didn't speak for a moment, "I wasn't going to—"

"Fire me?"

"N-no, you're not getting fired. We have to let you go."

Both still meant she was out of a job. Again.

"Why?" Not that it mattered, but she was curious how he would lie to her.

"I was trying to explain that. The budget—"

He went on about resources being tight, she knew that was an excuse. "I make people uncomfortable," she cut in.

He sighed. "It's not that...exactly. As you know it helps to work as a unit."

"I try my best."

"We know that, that's not the problem. We...we think you need time to focus on your health."

Rina stiffened. She hated whenever someone referred to that. "I am fine."

"Our job is very vigorous and perhaps—"

"You don't have to worry. I'm not going to say anything."

"What?"

"About you and Ivan. Your husband won't hear a word from me."

Julian's eyes grew wide and she realized she'd made a mistake. He didn't know she knew about his affair with the bread maker. It was a shame really. Rina really liked Peter. He always reminded her of someone—an actor or some celebrity she couldn't place. Peter and Julian had been together ten years, had two daughters, and his wealthy husband helped finance Julian's second entrepreneurial venture without question. Julian was a reason she knew she'd never marry. If Peter couldn't find someone who would be loyal to him, then she knew her odds were slim.

"Are you blackmailing me?"

Rina flexed her fingers wondering the best way to back away from such a hot topic. "No, I was just—"

"How much do you want?"

"I'm only explaining that you don't have to worry about me. You don't have to let me go because you're afraid I'll talk."

Julian tugged on his collar. "It was Peter's idea, not mine. He's worried you may not be able to hold up."

Peter wanted to get rid of her, not Julian? She'd misjudged him. He saw her as a liability instead of an asset. He was looking in the wrong place, but he'd find out soon enough. Of course Julian could be lying and perhaps they had to make budget cuts and he wanted to keep his lover so he'd convinced Peter that it was better to get rid of her. No matter the reason she was still out of a job.

"Come back in a couple months. I might be able to change his mind by then. It would be great to have you back."

Liar, liar, liar. You never want to see me again especially now that I know your secret. "Fine." She stood. "Can I ask a favor?"

He tugged on his collar again, looking as if she were

about to pull out a knife and press it against his throat. "Okay."

"Can I sit in the front dining area until closing? I won't do anything, I just want to sit there."

He blinked quickly then nodded. "Uh...sure."

"Thank you."

Minutes later she sat at one of the round tables and looked at the customers. There was plenty of traffic and people walking past outside the large windows where a painted bee obscured part of her view. The bakery was situated on a main street and near an office district. But she preferred to watch the people inside the bakery. She watched them eat. Most didn't pay attention to what they were putting in their mouths. They were distracted by other things, talking to each other, typing on a laptop, reading...then her gaze fell on a man who wasn't doing any of those things.

Instead he sat alone at a table and took one bite of a croissant, briefly closed his eyes, touched the bottom of his lip with his tongue and chewed. It was a sensual moment that made her lick her bottom lip too. This was a man who loved food, paid attention to it.

She knew she shouldn't stare, but she couldn't help watching him. She watched his jaw, his mouth, his lips, even his hands. One was wrapped in a bandage, the other large with long fingers. There was something familiar about him.

Her cell phone rang, tearing her attention away from him. She saw the number and sighed. "Yes, Amelia?"

"I left you like a thousand messages."

"What do you want?" Rina asked as she returned her gaze so she could continue to watch the man eat.

She knew him from somewhere, but she couldn't place him.

"I have an idea."

Amelia always had an idea. "Okay," Rina said, hoping she'd sound bored enough so that her cousin would leave her alone and not ask her for anything.

"But I need your help."

Hope denied. "Uh, huh."

"Please, Dad can't see me fail at something again. My last pastry chef quit and we've got a big order that could make or break us. Please, I'm begging you."

Amelia had run a failed boutique, gallery and now was trying to run a catering company because she thought it would be fun. Rina wasn't in the mood to indulge her cousin's latest whim. "I'll think about it."

"I know you have a job, but it's this Saturday and you don't work then, right? It'll only be a couple hours of your time. We're family. We're supposed to help out each other."

Rina watched the man touch the corner of his mouth with his tongue. The sight of his pink tongue made Amelia's voice seem very far away. "I'll call you back."

Her voice rose in a whine. "I don't have much time."

She could hear the panic in her cousin's voice and fought not to focus on it. Amelia tended to panic about a lot of things. "How much do you need?"

"I could go under in a week. That's what my accountant says."

"Okay."

"Okay? That means you'll do it?"

"It means I understand the problem."

"So you know you *have* to help me."

"I need to think a few things over first."

"What's there to think about?"

"I'll get back to you by tomorrow."

"Please. You owe me—"

Rina disconnected the phone and sighed. She didn't want to think about Amelia or being fired. She just wanted to watch this man. She could watch him all day.

"Can't take your eyes off of him either, huh?" Darlene said, taking a seat. She was one of the chattiest women Rina had ever met. The patrons loved her and every time she saw Rina she either had a big smile, a compliment or a story to share.

At first Rina had found Darlene's attention unnerving since few people took the time to talk to her until she realized Darlene talked to everyone and could hold up her end of a conversation with a tree if she had to.

Rina felt herself blush. "No, I—"

"Don't worry. The first time I saw him I did the same. He's gorgeous to look at, but that's all."

Rina frowned. "What do you mean?"

Darlene tapped the side of her head. "Not much going on up there, if you know what I mean."

Rina's frown increased because she didn't.

Darlene sighed, leaned forward and lowered her voice. "He's sort of a regular, okay? He doesn't come all the time, but he comes enough that I got to know what he likes and I learned a few things about him." She glanced at him with a faint wistful smile before she looked at Rina again. "He's sweet and funny, but he's one of the clumsiest men you could meet."

"Clumsy?"

"Yes, in less than a year he's had a black eye, a cut hand, a dog bite, a twisted ankle and broken finger."

"He sounds more unlucky than clumsy."

"He's walked into a door twice, cut his hand while cooking, got attacked by a golden retriever and has even fallen down the stairs. I call that clumsy." She clicked her tongue in pity. "What a waste. So what are you doing out here?"

"Just taking a break." She didn't want to tell her about being let go.

"Well, I'd better get back to work, I just wanted to warn you not to get your hopes up."

"Thanks," Rina said then pretended to look around the bakery and not stare at him. But she did. Because he was familiar. She knew him. How? From where?

He rubbed his forehead and then...

And then she knew.

It was *him!!* The one who'd given her a rose. The man she'd met in the hospital. He'd been there because...

A pair of scissors. Yes, she remembered that now. He'd been stabbed and he'd smiled.

That smile had bothered her and it still did. She looked at his bandaged hand. He was still getting hurt? Was he really that clumsy? Was it a cry for help? Was he involved in something dangerous?

Rina bit her lip and rose from her chair. She could at least say "Hi", perhaps even find out his name.

She started to walk over to him then stopped when she saw his wife come into the bakery. But this time when he saw her, Rina saw his body slightly stiffen.

He was on alert. Rina recognized the emotion because she'd been on alert most of her life. Especially with Aunt Sonia, but sometimes with the rest of her family too. She did her best not to upset anyone.

But why would the sight of his wife cause him to do that? She watched him smile, the smile was the same, a little more guarded than she remembered or maybe it had always been that way.

She saw his wife take his hand, tenderly. The same tender way she had when she'd picked him up from the hospital. But something seemed wrong. She couldn't see what. His wife said something to him; he nodded then said something in reply. She hesitated, sighed then nodded and stood. She tenderly touched his cheek before she left.

Rina waited several minutes for his wife to return, but she didn't. She felt her heart pick up pace as she stood again. This was her chance, perhaps her only chance, to talk to him. To find out his name.

She knew it was a risk. He might not remember who she was. But even if he didn't it would be nice to hear his voice again.

She sat down at his table, pointed at his bandaged hand and said,

"What is it this time? Scissors again?"

He stared at her startled. "What?"

"You probably don't remember me. You dropped an orange—"

He sat back and his face split into a wide grin. "Nooo, I can't believe it's you."

"You remember me?" she said pleased.

"Of course I remember you." He looked her up and down. "You made it out. I wasn't sure you would."

She didn't know why he'd been worried, but the thought made her happy.

"How are you doing?" he asked her, his voice as beautiful as she'd remembered.

Got kicked out of a gym, got laid off. "I'm fine."

He nodded. "Me too."

She shook her head. "No, you're not."

He blinked. This time he didn't look startled, he looked guarded and a little dangerous. "What do you mean?"

She pointed to his bandage again. "I told you to be careful with sharp objects."

He grinned and the dangerous look left his face. "I'm trying."

"Try harder." She leaned forward. "What happened?"

She expected him to tell her that it was none of her business, but instead he said, "An accident in the kitchen."

Perhaps it was the way he said it, or the look in her eyes, but something told her he was lying and then she knew. She knew he wasn't clumsy. She knew she'd seen the pattern before as a child with Mr. CC...

CHAPTER FIFTEEN

*R*ina had never seen somebody wear sunglasses on a rainy day. It was dark, almost like night, and yet Wendy came into the Star Moon Hotel and Resort kitchen wearing large sunglasses. It was strange that no one else seemed to notice. No one else asked her why.

"It's because of her superpower," Mr. CC once told eleven year old Rina as they walked along the beach after a long day. "She can have laser focus and burn things when the air is heavy with rain."

Rina nodded although she knew he was teasing her, his stories always tended to the fantastical. But Rina quietly wondered if he was right about Wendy's superpowers because Wendy's husband seemed to adore her even though she was ordinary looking and not very bright. He was a good looking man with an easy smile, and nice (he'd once offered her a lollipop) and came to pick Wendy up every day and take her home in his shiny blue car. Rina wanted to be with someone like that some-day. Belong to someone who would take her away.

He also gave Wendy lots of gifts. She showed off a new necklace; he had a bouquet of roses delivered, although Rina thought that was silly since there was no place to put them in the kitchen.

One day as Rina watched Wendy drive off with her husband she caught Mr. CC studying her. She felt her face burn and wondered what she'd done wrong. Before she could apologize, he said in a low voice, "You see all those pretty things Ms. Wendy gets?"

"Yes," Rina said with a note of awe. "They are so beautiful."

"True, true. But there's a price. You don't want a man like that. If your father hasn't told you yet, I will. You want a man who can keep money in his wallet, his lips off liquor and his hands at his side. Understood?"

Rina nodded even though she didn't. Her dad liked liquor and he never had any money, but he was a good person. But the look in Mr. CC's eyes let her know that his words were important. He was warning her. "I under-stand," she said.

He seemed pleased by her response and never mentioned it again. And there was no need to when Wendy moved away.

It was later, when Rina was in her early twenties that she finally got to understand the kind of man Mr. CC had been warning her away from. Her roommate, Maddy, had a loud laugh and a jewelry box full of earrings to adorn her eight piercings (four on each ear).

She was talented, bright and ambitious. Until she met

a man named Tyler in one of her university classes. Soon everything was all about Tyler. Tyler said this and Tyler said that. Rina half expected to meet a god when Maddy finally introduced him. He was a pleasant enough guy, majoring in Economics, a little shy with a soft voice.

And hard fists.

It had taken Rina a few months to realize that the bruises that had suddenly shown up on her roommate's arm weren't due to time spent at the gym.

But roses always followed, beautiful red roses. Roses like the ones Ms. Wendy used to get.

Rina started to hate the sight of them. But then she understood what she hadn't as a child—the sunglasses, the neck wrapped in a scarf, the wrist covered by a bandage and the lovely jewelry that always followed.

Tyler couldn't afford jewelry, he lived on a students' income so he splurged on teddy bears. Rina thought they were ridiculous but Maddy collected them like treasures. There was hardly enough room on the bed for her.

It was the day she saw a hole in the living room wall and Maddy curled up on the ground crying that she'd had enough. "Let's call the police."

"No, it's nothing. I made him angry. I'll pay for the wall."

"But he's dangerous."

Maddy made excuses for him and to her shame Rina let her. She didn't want to believe that her friend was truly so naive. She didn't want to believe that Tyler, who looked so normal, who'd picked up extra food items for her when she'd run out; Tyler, who was smart and funny...

How could he be a monster?

Her father could get loud, angry, break things but he never touched them, ever. He said no man would do that.

He'd been wrong.

When Tyler finally broke Maddy's collarbone, Rina called the police.

Maddy never forgave her for that. She called her filthy names before she left their apartment and they never spoke again.

Rina thought about Maddy and Wendy as she stared at this man with the bandaged hand and half-eaten croissant. She knew his secret. Knew that he wouldn't be happy that she knew, but couldn't hide it. Not from her.

The guarded posture was the same. In his sweet, doting wife Rina saw Tyler; she saw Wendy's husband. Charming, happy Mr. Wendy. Sweet, innocent looking Tyler.

Perhaps if she hadn't been blinded by his gender she would have noticed the pattern sooner. What had she missed at the hospital?

She remembered how eager he had been to reassure his wife. At first that had seemed sweet, now she knew it had been a means of survival. Survival against her rage. What was he living with?

Rina flexed her hand. She didn't care if she didn't see him again, like Maddy they always chose the one they loved over her, but she'd promised herself she'd never stand by and watch. She would do or say something. Everyone had a right to their choices. She had a right to speak her mind even if they didn't want to listen. Especially if they didn't want to listen.

Rina looked at the man. "I never got to know your name."

A shuttered look came over his face. "You don't need to know my name."

Her heart fell. She'd lost him. The connection that they'd had had been broken.

Perhaps because of that, because she felt she had nothing to lose, she rested her arms on the table and said, "When you got hurt, was your wife in the kitchen too?"

He froze. He became so still it frightened her. She'd guessed, only guessed what was going on, partly hoping she was wrong. Now she knew for certain.

"No," he said in a dark voice. A voice of warning. "I was alone."

"She will kill you one day. You don't have to believe me, but it's true."

His gaze turned onyx. For a moment Rina wondered if he was really the monster, if his wife had been defending herself. But then she remembered how his wife had wrapped her arm around his. It hadn't been doting, it had been possessive.

Rina lowered her voice. "Abuse is never okay."

"No one is abusing anyone. Do you know how tall I am? How much I weigh?"

"Doesn't matter."

"Of course it matters. I'm a big guy and she—"

"Uses weapons."

His jaw twitched. "It's not—"

"Maybe it's not as bad as it looks. Maybe a black eye here and there is no big deal, but if I came in looking like you, what would you think?"

He let out a breath and shook his head. "It's different. We're different."

"Because I'm a woman? Things like this aren't supposed to happen to guys? Do you know what century this is? Do you know that someone you love has no right to strike you with anything?"

He pushed back his chair and stood. "I came here to support my brother-in-law's business, I don't need this."

"Wait, Julian's your brother-in-law?"

"Excuse me," the man said before he pushed past her and left.

The pieces began to fall into place. Peter was his brother? No wonder Peter always reminded her of someone. He reminded her of *him*. This man. This man whose name she still didn't know, who was walking out of her life again.

But just as she had years ago, she followed him into the warm spring weather, scented with rain. However, this time, she'd let him know it.

CHAPTER SIXTEEN

To her relief the sidewalk wasn't very crowded and he hadn't walked very far. Rina ran after him and grabbed his coat sleeve. He spun around and faced her, his expression fierce as a bear. He really could hurt her if he wanted to. He could push her aside and ignore her, but he didn't. He glared at her, but when he spoke his voice remained soft, "Let go while I'm asking you nicely."

Her heart pounded in her ears, as she tightened her grip on his sleeve. "I really don't care if you hate me right now. I'm going to do you a favor and tell you what you don't want to hear. You deserve better. You deserve better than someone who hurts you and then pretends to be sorry."

"You don't know anything about her. She *is* sorry. She is—"

"Someone who breaks her promise that she won't do it again," Rina said. "That says she didn't mean it. That says you made her do it. A woman who spews out her hurt on you because of something that happened to her in the past, right? It's not fair, life isn't fair. No one deserves to be someone else's punching bag."

He opened his mouth, but the sound of his cell phone ringing interrupted him. He looked around, as if searching the crowd, before he grabbed Rina's hand and pulled her to the side of one of the buildings where they could hide out of sight, as if he were afraid they'd be seen. As every second passed the ringing of his phone seemed to grow louder.

Finally he answered it. "Yeah, hi...I sound out of breath? No, I'm still at the bakery." He stared at Rina as if daring her to contradict him. "I'll be leaving soon. Uh... huh...n-no you don't have to worry about me."

Rina watched and listened to him soothing his wife with his lies. While his words were false his feelings were real. He really cared about her. He wanted to protect her, protect his marriage.

It was at that moment, as he awkwardly held the phone in his bandaged hand, while his good hand held her still that it happened. His palm felt hot against her skin. She didn't know why he held on, wasn't sure if he'd forgotten that she was there or was he afraid she'd say something that his wife could hear, but he didn't let go and it was then that she fell in love with him.

Because in the alley she saw a man who was strong and tender and loyal and brave. Dangerously so. She loved him because he was an easy man to love. He was safe and out of reach. Loving him wouldn't mean risking anything. She already knew he could never be hers. She'd never think of dreaming that big. But loving him felt right.

She wanted to kiss his cheek, cradle his hand, tell him that love didn't have to be painful.

"Uh...huh," he continued. "I'll be there soon. Me too. Bye." He tucked his phone away inside his coat.

"You don't have to be ashamed of loving her," Rina said before he could speak. "But don't let that love keep you under her control. I know this. I know this because I've been hurt and tried to get someone to love me who never will. You can—"

His grip tightened. "If you mention this to anyone—"

"There's nothing to be ashamed of." That was what the counselors were always telling her and she believed it.

His brows shot up; he released his hold. "Ashamed? Are you kidding me?" He held up his bandaged hand. "This is downright humiliating. I know my marriage isn't perfect. I know..." He bit his lip. "But who am I supposed to talk to? Who would really understand? Who wouldn't laugh at me? You think it's easy to admit that—"

"You're being abus—"

He pressed a hard finger to her lips. "Don't say it. I'm not. It's just a few arguments that get out of hand. I could leave anytime."

"But you don't because you're afraid she'd fall apart. That she might hurt herself, blame herself. She's been abandoned before and you promised you wouldn't do that."

"Yes, I did. I made a vow. You don't know what she's been through or what I've been through. I don't break promises easily."

"No, and you can keep this promise as long as you don't mind dying."

He sniffed. "She won't kill me."

"She stabbed you with a pair of scissors."

He lowered his gaze.

"Two years ago you got lucky. What if she strikes and hits a major vessel or organ by accident? She won't mean to do it, she never does, but it won't matter because you'll be on the ground bleeding to death."

He stared at her. "That's enough."

Rina stared back. "Don't tell me. Tell her," she said then turned to walk away, but he didn't let her.

He grabbed her wrist and spun her back to face him and for a moment she was afraid. Afraid that she'd pushed him too far. That the inner hurt and rage that swirled within him would be released on her.

"You want to talk about dying? What about you?"

"What about me?"

"You think I'm the only one with secrets? You think I don't know what put you in the hospital?"

She trembled. "I don't have any secrets."

He lifted her wrist, causing the sleeve of her blouse to fall down revealing her bare arm. "What did you eat today? Anything?"

She tried to pull free. "Let me go."

"Why do you hate yourself?"

"I don't hate myself."

"When you look in the mirror what do you see?"

Her counselor had asked her that same question once. She'd lied and told her that she'd seen someone who was capable and daring. "I don't see anything."

He released her wrist and stared at her. She inwardly smiled, pleased she'd gotten the reaction she'd hoped for. She turned to leave, but his arm shot out and blocked her.

"Explain."

Rina took a deep, steadying breath. She had pushed him too far, she'd crossed a line she shouldn't have. He wouldn't hurt her physically, but he'd hurt her with words and she wasn't in the mood for it. "Forget I said anything. I'm sorry I made you angry—"

He didn't move. He didn't even blink. He just continued to stare at her. "Explain."

She swallowed. "There's nothing to see." I don't really exist, she wanted to say. But she couldn't tell him that because he would think she was crazy. He wouldn't understand how she lived in the world. How many people lived. How you could be alive and invisible at the same time. A man like him wouldn't know what it was like. She sighed and rubbed her arm where his hand had been. "Never mind." She shook her head. "It's your life and I had no right—"

"No, you didn't, but you spoke up anyway. I don't know why. I just—" He bit his lip. "I don't listen to hypocrites."

"I'm not a hypocrite," Rina said.

"You talk about living when you're dying every day."

"We're all slowly dying."

"Some faster than others. Do you have any friends? What do you do for a living? Do you really think you can keep this up? You look like a skeleton."

Rina winced as his words struck her. He'd ripped her

bare, raw. As if he had the power to rip her flesh from her bones and expose her.

She had no friends, she only worked, but no one, not colleagues or acquaintances, had ever said that to her before. They'd mentioned her weight in passing, told her that she was a little too thin, but nothing like this. His words hurt but she still loved him. She loved him because he could actually see her. She wasn't invisible to him.

She shrugged, pretending not to be bothered. "It's just the way I'm built. I did eat something this morning." She wanted to tell him that she was better now. That she'd learned that ghosts had to eat too.

He rested his hands on his hips. "You know what it's like, don't you? You know what it's like to not want to be around anymore. When I was a kid..." He shook his head. "Doesn't matter. Truth is, I want you around." He bit his lip. "I don't know why because you see too much and irritate me and..." He took a deep breath. "But I do. So let's make a promise to each other. From this moment on we'll both choose to live. Whatever it takes."

"But I—"

"But we'll do it as an exchange. You live for me and I'll live for you."

She frowned. "Your life is worth more than mine."

For a moment he looked sad. "No, it's not. And this will prove it. You live your life as if it were mine, and I'll live it as if it were yours. As if we were both given a second chance. If my life depended on you how would you live it? Would you make the same choices? Live the same way?"

It was a challenge. At twenty-seven she was being

given a chance to start again. She had nothing to lose just like when she'd first met him. She'd had no job or friends then either.

But more than herself she thought of him. If she said yes, he might leave his wife, he might realize that he deserved better. He could live a future she could only dream about.

"Okay, I'll do it. You promise you'll do the same?"

His jaw twitched, he nodded but didn't speak.

"Say it."

"I will."

She smiled. "Good." She was so relieved that she impulsively hugged him. He felt solid and warm.

He gently, but firmly pushed her away, making it clear he didn't want to be touched. Especially by her. They weren't friends, just strangers who shared secrets. He pushed her forward. "Go. Don't look back, just go." He shook his head. "Don't look at me. I mean it. Go."

"Someone once told me that the moment you make up your mind about something, things start to change."

"I said go."

"You can start to be happy now. You don't have to be sad anymore."

He shoved her again. "Get out of here."

This time she listened.

She could feel him watching her as she left, hoping he did. She could also feel her heart opening up a little with each step she took away from him. She decided to love him even more. She decided that it would be a love she'd guard and treasure. She'd love him because his wife couldn't. She'd love him because it felt nice to love someone.

Even a semi-stranger she'd never meet again. She didn't know how she would move forward, but then the answer came when she thought of Amelia. She pulled out her cell phone and dialed. The moment Amelia picked up she said, "I'll help you this weekend."

"Great because I have an amazing idea..."

CHAPTER SEVENTEEN

She was wrong.

Warren wanted to run after her and shake her. Tell her that. But then he'd be lying because she was right. He did hate her. He hated her for uncovering his secret and forcing him to face it.

He hated her because she didn't know him and yet she cared.

He hated that he let her catch up with him, let her grab his sleeve, let her hold onto him.

But what was worse was when he held onto her. When his cell phone rang, his first instinct was to ignore it. He'd tell his wife that he'd turned it off, or left it on the table. He'd come up with an excuse, instead...instead he'd panicked and grabbed this woman's hand. And he didn't let go. He didn't let go even though he knew he should. Because she knew his secret, she could expose him.

He didn't let go even as he lied. He rarely lied like that anymore.

It was why he'd married Myra. Most of his childhood had been made up of lies. Lies to his mother. Lies to his teachers. Lies to the reporters. Lies to the world.

He was supposed to have left that all behind him.

But he couldn't escape it. It wasn't just a vow that kept him with his wife. It was his pride. His marriage couldn't fail, he'd risked too much to make it happen. His world would crumble without it. His identity too.

Suddenly he heard Mahler's Ninth Symphony, a piece he'd heard performed many times, but this time he felt the melancholy piece more than before. His fingers absently moved in accordance to the notes that filled his head, the sound of the violins and cellos, the orchestra's soft entrance.

He hadn't had a sad life like Mahler, he hadn't lost seven brothers and sisters to sickness, he hadn't lost a child, or been brought up by a father who'd been cruel or had an invalid mother.

Nor had he dealt with sickness that had been a lingering threat, Mahler had to face illness while he was composing this symphony. He'd been diagnosed with a weak heart and told he only had a short time to live.

Death lingered within every note, this piece was his final goodbye, which was why the end of the piece dies out to nothingness...like one's last breath.

Warren felt it now. Like he was dying.

It would be his second death. The first had come when he'd turned away from music.

Music had been his entire life and existence. His father had been a renowned operatic baritone, his mother a cellist. His brother Peter was the only non-musical person in the family to his parents' dismay, but Warren's arrival more than made up for it.

He'd started improvising on the piano at two, achieved global fame by six and made his debut with the Chicago Symphony by ten. By twenty he'd traveled from Zurich to New Zealand, played Mendelssohn to Mozart, composed piano etudes and released them through a major label before experimenting with recording songs and letting people access them directly online (to his parents' annoyance).

As he grew the pressure did too. He had no time for himself, no time to be the artist he wanted to be. As much as he loved his mother, she gave him little space. Hiring Myra as his new manager had been his mini rebellion.

Quitting music and marrying Myra at twenty had been an even bigger one. But at the time it had felt right. She understood him, she supported him. She was one of the few people outside of his family he felt he could trust.

He'd made more than enough money to live on and with his brother's help he'd managed to invest in two companies that had been profitable and allowed him a very comfortable lifestyle. He found the life of a businessman boring but sensible. It gave them a lifestyle of travel his wife enjoyed.

They'd built a life together. It was his ticket to freedom.

Her tempers were the price he had to pay. The first time she'd thrown a glass at him, he'd been too stunned to believe it. Then he laughed.

When she'd thrown the second glass, he stopped laughing.

He explained it all away. It wasn't always bad. He knew he wasn't the easiest person to live with. Although his mother had been strict at least he knew she loved him, his wife hadn't had the same upbringing. She'd basically raised herself with a mostly absent mother and a father she'd never met. Warren desperately wanted to make her happy. Wanted to have the happy home life he'd imagined others had. Not one filled with rules and regulation and endless practices, heavy whacks with a cane on the shoulder if he got a note wrong.

There were times when he hated playing the piano so much that he imagined breaking his fingers by slamming the car door on them, or cutting them with a knife.

He didn't have those thoughts anymore. He wasn't forced to play or do anything he didn't want to anymore.

Except that was a lie.

Every day he was being forced to pretend that nothing was wrong.

But this woman—this tiny stranger—was telling him he had a choice and for the first time, in a long time, he wanted to believe it. He was tired of his shame, his misery.

He let Mahler's Ninth Symphony fade from his mind and shift to something else. Something he'd let himself forget.

Mahler hadn't always been sad. He loved nature and life, which flowed through his music as much as his anger at his father's brutality and sadness of his loss and illness.

Warren felt a renewed hope he'd let fade.

He realized he wanted to live.

The truth was he hadn't let go of her because he didn't want to.

He hadn't forgotten about her. He'd thought about her over the past two years more than he should have.

He sank against the wall. She'd told him there was no shame in loving his wife. But the biggest shame was that she'd become a habit. He'd stopped loving her years ago.

He'd stopped loving life as well.

Warren took a deep breath and pushed himself from the wall.

He didn't know her name, but he gripped his good hand into a fist, closed his eyes and made a silent plea.

"I don't know who you are, why you cared, but one day I hope to meet you again and prove I was worth it..."

He left the alley with a renewed purpose knowing the road ahead of him wouldn't be easy, but the memory of her touch, her fierce gaze and painful words would lead him through and he was determined to make it. His long buried love of music rose within him once more and he felt the desire to compose again...on his terms.

PART III

**"If you don't like the road you're walking,
start paving another one."**

Dolly Parton

CHAPTER EIGHTEEN

"Oh my God it worked."

"What worked?" Rina asked absently. They both sat in the offices of Private Pastry Chef Inc, the idea Amelia had come up with seven years ago and Rina had helped her build. Amelia had decided to stop catering and run a business that specialized in serving a select audience—mostly small conventions and small business owners—who ordered specialty desserts as gifts for clients or as special accents for exclusive events.

While Amelia took care of the marketing, Rina took care of the menu. She wanted to get back to basics—butter, flour, sugar, milk, yogurt and not depend on cake mixes, frozen pie crusts or premade tubs of frosting. Instead, every client could be assured of homemade pie crusts and puff pastries, and hand rolled croissants.

The business had grown so profitable that Rina found herself doing more non-baking tasks than she'd wanted since Amelia, although clever with ideas, had a poor time always carrying them out.

Today she and Amelia were going over the schedule for two forthcoming events that were too close together to give their staff adequate time to prepare. But while Rina was looking over the calendar, Amelia was staring at her cell phone.

At thirty-three Amelia didn't look much changed from when she was six, except her beauty was even more evident now with a lovely round face, dark hair that fell to her shoulders, curvy figure dressed in a black top and red skirt. Making her the face of Private Pastry Chef had been a strategic and profitable idea. There was a picture of her standing in the kitchen, smiling while wearing a double breasted white chef's jacket posted on the wall. She gave their business the "personal" touch that clients had come to expect although Amelia didn't bake. She'd taken a course where she'd failed miserably, and truly had little interest in the day to day operations of how the business was run. However, being the planner and detailed person she was, Rina made sure that wasn't a problem.

Before she'd been able to work with Amelia fulltime, she'd worked at a bakery where she'd been forced to make tart shells only a fraction bigger than a nickel for nearly eight months straight until her eyes started to cross. This was a big improvement and suited her more than she thought, although there were times she wondered if she were meant for something more.

Which was why, starting next week, Rina would begin to train a replacement for her non-baking duties, because she'd grown bored of running the company instead of baking and was eager to embark on something new. Even though she wasn't quite sure what that was yet.

"I can't believe it," Amelia said in awe. "It really worked."

"Can't believe what?" Rina asked, sounding bored.

"Okay, don't get mad."

Rina paused and lifted her head from her computer screen. Those words were always a bad sign. "What have you done?"

"It's not as bad as last time."

"When you promised a potential customer raspberry croissants even though you know we only offer almond, plain or chocolate?"

Amelia rolled her eyes. "I said I was sorry."

"When you almost got us locked into a three year lease with a landlord—"

"That was an honest mistake."

"Who thought Private Pastry Chef was a euphemism for prostitutes?"

"The location was cheap, it had a big kitchen, which you said you wanted, and since we deliver most of our products I didn't think it mattered much."

"It matters when you're leasing a building situated between a massage parlor with a guard outside the door and a bookstore with hardly any books in it."

"It was an honest mistake." Amelia held up her hands before Rina could argue. "This isn't that bad."

Rina sat back and folded her arms. "I'm listening."

She cleared her throat. "You know those chocolate flowers you were making the other night?"

"Yes."

"The ones you let me try?"

"Yes."

"The ones with mixed nuts and dried fruit—"

Rina let her arms fall. "Get to the point, Amelia."

"You made so much and I thought they shouldn't go to waste...so... I sent them to a client."

"You did what! Those were experiments."

"I told you not to get mad. Besides they were delicious."

"I told you not to do that. I thought I could trust you."

"I've never done it before, but...I was desperate, I wanted to give him something special."

"Why?"

"Because—" She put a hand over her chest and sighed. "He's amazing. Gorgeous doesn't even begin to describe him and he's so smart and—"

"What does that have to do with the chocolate flowers?"

"I'm getting to that. He looked me up, Rina. Personally. He did a search online to find out about me."

"So what?"

"Will you just listen? He attended some sort of gaming convention where the hostess gave our croissants to their speakers as a special thank you. He told me that he was so impressed he asked the coordinator who'd delivered them and when he found out about our company he had to meet me.

"I mean...I didn't think much about it when he called.

He had a nice voice and all but we know gamers are geeks, right? So I didn't think…" She bit her lip. "He said he wanted to place an order but before he did he wanted to come down to our office and meet me personally. That he'd read my background story and how he'd gone after his dream like I had and while he was talking I looked him up and… Oh. My. God."

Rina rested her chin in her hand, bored. "I still don't care."

Amelia scrolled through her cell phone. "He's sizzling hot. Get me a firehose gorgeous. If you saw him—"

Rina waved her away. "You're still not making sense."

"I swear I almost started drooling."

Rina tapped the desk with impatience. "Get to the point."

"He came here and he was so…sexy. We flirted a bit and then he asked me if he could try something I'd made that wasn't on the menu. I told him that I'd send him something special. He said he'd look forward to it while he also placed an order for four of our Danish pastries. Once he left, I panicked. I couldn't think of anything to make for him and then…"

"You thought about the chocolate flowers," Rina finished with a sigh.

"They were right there and they were meant to be eaten. They were perfect. So perfect that he told me he loved them and he invited me to dinner."

"Congratulations. But don't ever—"

"I'm not finished."

"There's more?"

"I went out with him and it was amazing. Fireworks amazing. I'd never had a connection with a man like that before. And after..." She stopped and Rina filled in the blank. Amelia had been very hurt about her last relationship ending due to her boyfriend's cheating. "I'm sure he felt the same. We've gone out a couple more times, each better than the last and he kept hinting at wanting something special from me again. I thought if I gave him something basic that he'd stop asking so I took one of those simple cupcakes you like to make for the staff and I gave it to him."

"And?" Rina pressed when Amelia fell silent.

"He's traveling to New York for the weekend and wants to take me with him. And I desperately want to go."

"So go."

Amelia looked miserable. "I said I'd make something special for him and sort of said it would be a monthly surprise. I just heard back from him. He loves the idea."

"Monthly?"

"I know, I said it before I could take it back."

"You can still take it back. Tell him you're busy. If you're seriously dating he'll understand."

"But he was so happy, I'd hate to disappoint him. Please help me."

"What am I supposed to do?" When Amelia sent her a silent plea, Rina shook her head. "No."

She pressed her hands together. "Please. You're always testing out new things, baking like there's no tomorrow. This will hardly be work for you. You're always wanting me to taste what you're doing this would give you a second perspective."

Rina liked the idea. Amelia was right. She did have many things she wanted to try and this would give her a chance to try them on someone who clearly had more than just a casual appreciation for food. Amelia wasn't as specific. As long as it was sweet, full of cream or oozing with frosting, she was a lost woman. But this man...this man could take her culinary skills to another level.

"Okay, I'll do it."

Amelia squealed in delight.

"On one condition. You have to make sure to tell me specifically what he likes and doesn't like about each dish."

"Okay."

"Ask him and write down what he says."

She nodded. "I will."

"And I'll only do this for three months."

"Six."

"Three."

"Six would be so much better, plus it would give me a chance to improve my cooking—"

"Baking."

"Too. There's no way I could do it in three months."

Rina sighed. "Fine. Six, but no more."

Amelia wiggled in her seat like a happy child. "Ooh a different dessert every month." She clapped her hands in delight. "Wasn't this a good idea after all? We're both getting something out of it. I'll even come up with a reason to drop by his house and make a personal delivery." She giggled. "Won't that be fun?"

"Sure," Rina said without the same enthusiasm. "But I'm still leaving the company and remember I'm only doing this for six months. After that you're on your own."

Amelia flashed a superior grin. "Don't worry, by that time I'll make sure he's so in love with me the food won't matter."

CHAPTER NINETEEN

*I*f heaven was a dish, this was it.

Warren carefully set down his spoon and stared at his now empty dish, which only minutes ago had been a *crème brulee* topped with a dollop of fresh whipped cream and strawberries.

The flavors and sensations continued to hum within him. Just as they had the first day he'd tasted Amelia's food.

He could remember that day, almost three months ago, vividly. He'd been excited but tired after the gaming conference that he'd attended as a speaker to encourage underrepresented youngsters and university aged students to join the multi-billion dollar video game industry. He had a deadline he had to get back to and was hurrying to the exit when the organizer had presented him with a chocolate croissant. He absently thanked her before heading towards the exit. He was halfway to his destination when he decided to take a quick bite.

And nearly walked into a wall.

The soft pastry gripped him in a sensual assault. He stopped to take another bite to make sure. No, he wasn't imaging it. This was nothing like he'd had before.

And yet it was. He knew this feeling. This taste. It wasn't just familiar or similar to something he'd had before. It was much more than that. It was a feeling, like coming home. He hurried back and found the organizer and said, "Where did you get this?"

She looked startled. "What?"

He motioned to the croissant. "Who gave this to you?"

"Is there a problem?"

"There's no problem," he said quickly, sorry he'd caused her any dismay. "Just give me a name."

"They're amazing, aren't they?"

More than that. All he could do was nod. He didn't care about discussing it. He just needed a name.

And he soon got it. Amelia Parker, owner of Private Pastry Chef.

At home he looked up everything he could about her. He needed to find out more. He looked the company up and it seemed like a regular business with a classy, professional website and attractive owner. He had to meet her.

There was something special about the food, about her backstory. When he finally got the chance to speak to her she was a little distant on the phone, but he didn't blame her. He was a stranger and she was likely used to people gushing about her food. He knew he had to make her realize he was different. Telling her he wanted to place an order, but that he had to meet her first had been reckless and he wouldn't have been surprised if she'd turned him down, but over the course of their brief conversation her voice had warmed to him and given him the confidence that he wouldn't frighten her.

He told her how he was amazed that there was nothing industrial about her food, that it felt homemade.

"That's what we're about," she said with a deep throated laugh that caused his pulse to quicken. "Everything is made from fresh and real ingredients on site."

He knew that, he knew about ad copy, but he hadn't believed it, if he hadn't tasted them for himself. It was as if every bite had been personalized. What they'd managed to do had been extraordinary. Or had he imagined it?

Meeting her had confirmed that she was even more striking than her picture online, but eating one of the Danish pastries he'd ordered...?

At first he sat in his kitchen and stared at the Danish pastries sitting inside the cardboard box.

He sat and stared at them not expecting to be impressed. He was hoping for too much. They couldn't be as good as the croissant.

Then he took a bite of the Danish and he was once again wrapped in a crisp brown pastry, his body seized in a slow, sensual seduction.

How was this possible? How could one tiny bite do this to him? But one bite wasn't enough. He took another and each bite built on each other, he didn't feel overwhelmed. The flavors complimented each other, the sensation was intoxicating.

Amelia gave credit to the other chefs who worked

with her, those she'd helped train in her method. And he would have accepted her reasoning that it was just how everything from her kitchen was. But then he tried the chocolate flower she'd added to his order.

One bite and he was a lost man.

He knew it wasn't just a simple method. A culinary trick that could be taught. It was her. *She* made all the difference.

He wanted her all to himself.

And now he had her. Amelia grinned as she sat across the table from him. She'd invited him over to her apartment to try her latest treat.

"Did you like it?" she said with a sly grin.

"You know you don't have to ask that."

"Tell me what you liked."

He laughed. This part he liked best about her. Every time he ate one of her desserts she asked him a series of questions. "Everything was perfect."

"It couldn't have been perfect."

"It was. I'd only—" He stopped. He hated criticizing anything, especially something so minor.

"What? What didn't you like?"

"It's not that I didn't like it. It's...the strawberries were a tad overpowering, perhaps if you had mixed berries instead that would have been a more complementary combination."

She furiously typed her notes into her phone. He would never have thought she'd have this side to her. She was pretty carefree about everything else. Even a little scatterbrained. At times so much so that he wondered how she ran such a successful business. But it was moments like this, when she took careful notes and paid attention to every detail that he realized the side of her he'd grown to love.

CHAPTER TWENTY

"Mixed berries?" Rina said to make sure she had read Amelia's notes correctly. She was in her kitchen cleaning up when she'd called her cousin the following day to find out how things had gone.

"Yes."

"He wasn't more specific than that?"

"I forgot to ask."

"You promised me you would—"

"I forgot okay. I will next time." She paused. "Better yet, you can hear me ask him tomorrow when he comes to pick me up. We're going to—"

"Why do I have to meet him?"

"You will eventually. Besides he wants to meet you."

"Why?"

"He's interested about the business and he has some questions that I really can't answer so I told him my business partner could talk to him. And that would be you."

"Why is he asking questions about the business?"

"I don't know. It's just the way he is. He said his brother-in-law." Amelia paused and Rina could hear her nails tapping against a table or something hard. "Or was it his *ex* brother-in-law. Hmm... Anyway, someone he knows or used to know once owned a bakery or something and it made him curious how we managed to be so successful in a market that seems crowded. It's no big deal. Just say hi and try not to drool."

"He should probably meet your family before he meets me."

"You *are* family."

Rina suppressed a laugh. *Could have fooled me.* "I guess I'd hope to meet him after you'd started baking for him on your own."

"I will soon. I'm getting better. And let's get this straight he likes your cooking—"

"Baking."

"But he loves *me*."

Rina sighed. Her cousin was right. It was a minor deception. A bunch of sweet desserts wouldn't keep a man by a woman's side for this long. Amelia had a lot to offer a man.

But the following day she didn't have time to think about meeting Amelia's boyfriend when one of the chefs called in sick and she had to take over. But she enjoyed being in the commercial kitchen again. By the end of the day almost every part of her body ached. She'd never felt so alive.

Amelia rushed into the kitchen as Rina cleared up. "Warren's here."

Rina nodded. "Okay. I'll wash my hands and then—"

Amelia stopped her, her eyes wide. "You can't meet him like that."

"Why not?"

"You look like a chef. I'm supposed to be the chef, remember? You're the businessperson."

"I'll just tell him I'm learning from you. He won't notice."

"But—"

"Relax. I know what I'm doing."

She walked through the door and stopped when she saw him.

Her smile froze in place.

Nine years ago he'd given her a yellow rose.

Seven years ago she'd faced him in an alley and they'd both made a promise.

She never imagined she'd see him again.

But there was no recognition in his eyes. There was not even a tiny glimmer in any part of his expression that made her think he knew her.

Had he forgotten about her? Was she that insignificant, unextraordinary? Was she foolish to think that she had been someone memorable in his life? He'd likely met hundreds, possibly thousands of people in the years that had passed between them but because she'd chosen him to love she remembered everything about him, the shape of his jaw, his lips, the breadth of his shoulders, his hands.

But to him, she was a stranger. No, not a stranger. Amelia's business partner. Nothing more.

Rina pushed down the pain. Her life as a ghost began again. Who she truly was, was invisible to him. She maintained her smile and said, "Nice to meet you. Amelia has told me a lot."

He laughed. "All good I hope." For some reason the sound of his laughter sounded forced, hollow, insincere. Like the laugh of a politician or sales clerk. He hadn't laughed like that in the past. His laughter had been more genuine, filling her heart with warmth. Even his eyes were different. The warmth was gone. But he was a different person now. No one could suspect what he'd gone through. Or perhaps she'd imagined it. Perhaps this was the man he'd always been and she hadn't realized it. He had remembered her from the hospital, when they'd met again at the bakery. What was so different now?

"Of course," Amelia said with a giggle, wrapping her arm tighter around his. "Especially how much you like my cooking."

Baking, Rina wanted to correct her, then her heart grew cold as she came to a painful realization. Not only was Warren Amelia's new boyfriend, Rina had been baking for *him* all this time. She didn't know how to feel. Happy and terrified. Happy that he'd loved her work, she'd imagined feeding him before and she had, but now...now that would never come to be. She had been helping him fall in love with somebody else.

"She's an angel," he said. And for the first time his eyes were as she'd remembered, affectionate, a little mischievous. "Every bite sends me to heaven."

Amelia giggled again. "The way to a man's heart, right?"

"Speaking of food, I'd like to one day treat you ladies to lunch. So—"

She couldn't stay any longer. The less than fifteen minutes in his company hurt enough, she couldn't imagine more time than that. Time where Amelia would continue to giggle and hold on to him like a gift she didn't want to share; him smiling back at her with that inane—was it just her imagination?—smile. It was best that he and Amelia be alone. Three being a crowd and all that. "Thank you," Rina said. "But I can't. I have to go. Again, it was nice meeting you."

"Sure." Did he look relieved?

Amelia's face fell. "But, Rina—"

"I don't want to pressure her," Warren quickly said. "It's was a pleasure meeting you too."

Rina nodded and for a moment their eyes met, his dark gaze pinning hers, and she knew his words were a lie.

CHAPTER TWENTY-ONE

"*W*hat's wrong with you?"

Since Rina had been asking herself that question most of her life she didn't have a ready answer when Amelia showed up on her doorstep that evening looking like thunder. "Don't you like him?"

"I don't know what you're talking about?"

Amelia pushed past her and walked over to the couch and sat down. "I'm talking about how you treated Warren. You left so abruptly when he was trying to be nice."

Rina sat in front of her. Once Amelia settled in, getting her to leave would take effort. "I had errands to run."

"You could have done them later. I told you he was coming by. He was so upset that he canceled our date."

Rina's brows shot up. "Really?"

"He got a phone call and then told me we'd have to reschedule, but I could tell he was upset."

"I'm sure he was busy," Rina said but Amelia wasn't listening.

"Well to make it up to him," she said. "I told him I'd make him something special."

"Good for you. Make him a simple tart."

Amelia shook her head. "Not me, you."

"I don't have the time."

"You owe me."

"I don't owe you anything."

"He really felt awkward after you left like that. If I knew you'd behave like that I wouldn't have introduced you."

"It doesn't matter what he thinks of me, you're the one he's dating. You're going to have to keep practicing your baking skills, I promised only a set number of dishes."

Amelia folded her arms and studied her. "You're certainly in a strange mood. He was too. I don't care. I don't like it when my baby's upset." She stood. "Find the time, this weekend I'll come pick it up."

Rina followed her to the front door. "But I don't—"

"Make sure it's delicious," Amelia demanded before she walked out the door. She turned to her. "And don't disappoint me," she said before she left.

Rina closed the door and fell into her couch. She half considered not making anything. She could imagine Amelia's haughty face arriving at her apartment door and the satisfaction it would bring her to say that she hadn't baked anything. Amelia would look shocked and briefly Rina would feel triumphant, but then her cousin's face would crumble and she'd tell her how hurt she was, that she'd promised Warren and Rina didn't want to force her cousin to show up empty handed. So she'd make something easy, reminding herself that she only had two more months to go before the six months were up and her cousin's relationship was solid, her baking skills had hopefully improved, and Rina was free to stop helping her.

Rina went to her kitchen.

But for the first time in her life she couldn't bake. The kitchen felt foreign. Her mind blank. She couldn't think of any ideas. She didn't want to make something for him. Knowing who he really was (not some phantom Rina had made up in her mind) made baking difficult. Those cold eyes, that tight jaw. He was the one who'd been criticizing her food? He was the one whose opinion she'd eagerly listened to?

She expected her heart to turn cold, to freeze any remaining feelings for him to ice. Instead her heart burned, her skin burned. She felt as if she were on fire.

How could he have forgotten her so completely, why did she care so much? She'd wanted him to live, he'd left his wife and his past behind. That was all that he owed her. Their promise hadn't bound them together with anything more than words. He'd fulfilled his.

And she hers. They'd both lived.

He hadn't asked for her love, she'd given it freely, thinking she'd never see him again.

She'd been terribly wrong.

Rina rested her hands on the kitchen counter and sighed, desperately wishing the ache in her heart would subside. It gripped like a physical pain. She couldn't bake for him now.

Not yet at least.

Not until she got over this hurt.

The hurt of Mr. CC leaving and not having a chance to say goodbye.

The hurt of Brian standing her up and pretending he hadn't.

The hurt of loving a stranger who didn't remember she'd ever existed.

Rina pushed herself from the counter and called Amelia.

"I can't do it," she told her.

"But you have to. I told him I would—"

"You're good at lying. Come up with a reason."

"That's not fair. I can't believe you're doing this to me! Are you jealous? Is that it?"

"I told you I was busy."

"You're always busy. Why is it different now? What's gotten into you?"

"Bye Amelia." She disconnected and let the phone ring and ignored all the text alerts.

She wouldn't be swayed. She wouldn't let her cousin manipulate her. She'd do only the designated desserts and no more.

Amelia tried to make her feelings known at work, she pouted and sulked. After a week of Rina ignoring her they went back to business as usual.

Or so Rina thought until Aunt Sonia arrived at her apartment. Aunt Sonia never visited her. So she stood stunned when she opened the door one evening and saw her aunt standing there. Time had only made her more striking, given an extra haughtiness to her features.

"Aren't you going to invite me in?" she said.

Rina mutely took a step back.

Aunt Sonia cast her critical eye over Rina's simple décor (the expensive pastel green couch Amelia had gotten bored of, the elegant planter Aunt Lauren had bought duplicates of) before she took a seat.

"Would you like some tea?"

Aunt Sonia clasped her hands in her lap. "I won't be staying long. You know why I'm here."

She couldn't believe Amelia would stoop this low. To call Aunt Sonia because she won't make a special dessert for her boyfriend? Had she really revealed their plan to the family? Before Rina could defend herself, Aunt Sonia said, "You have no right leaving Amelia in the lurch."

"What?"

"All that this family has given you and this is how you repay them? By forcing Amelia to run the business by herself?"

That was what this was about? Her leaving the Private Pastry Chef? Amelia had been complaining about it?

Rina sighed. "She'll be fine. The business will be fine. The new manager is—"

"Not you. Amelia is...special. She needs special attention. How can you be sure that—"

"I don't want to work at the company anymore."

Aunt Sonia tightened her lips. "Do you have any idea how much that facility cost your aunt and uncle? The sacrifice they've had to make? You owe them your life."

Rina shifted her gaze. Her aunt would never let her forget that. It didn't matter that she'd offered to repay Uncle Timothy and that he'd refused. That she'd let Amelia have a large stake in the business, although Rina did most of the work. That whatever financial burden her aunt constantly reminded her of, didn't actually reveal itself in any way. The family still maintained a comfortable lifestyle, Carla achieved her graduate degree and worked in her father's lab and her uncle at times grumbled more about Amelia's different business ventures than Rina's rehab costs.

But she'd learned over the years that as kindhearted as Uncle Timothy was he couldn't be trusted, that Aunt Lauren would rather fret over the delivery of a new couch than listen to five minutes of what Rina had to say, that Aunt Sonia truly ran the Parker household and that was the way her aunt and uncle preferred it.

Rina faced her aunt's cold gaze, feeling the sting of her icy words and wanted to scream at her. *What did I do to make you hate me? What can I do to make you stop?*

It was too much. Warren not remembering her and her aunt reminding her that she had no right to her own life. She had no right to her own existence.

She felt the tingling of unshed tears and fought to stop them. She promised herself that Aunt Sonia would never see her cry.

"If Amelia needs any help, she knows how to reach me." She took a deep breath. "But I'm not changing my mind." She stood. "If there's nothing else..."

Aunt Sonia smiled. "Amelia told me you're jealous." She nodded at Rina's stunned expression. "That's understandable of course. You lack in so many areas she doesn't, your soul is a field ripe for the poisonous seed to take root. But I have hope for you, I always have hope so I want you to listen to me carefully, *for where envy and selfish ambition exist, there is disorder and every kind of evil.* Guard your heart and mind of the tempter's influence."

"I am not jealous or envious of my cousins. I am truly happy for them."

She clicked her tongue. "You almost sound convincing."

"I'm telling the truth. I want a life of my own."

She stood and wagged her finger. "But one day you'll go too far and you'll end up with no one to turn to. Think about that. Think where your arrogance and stubbornness will take you," she said before she left.

Rina swore and grabbed her cell phone and furiously sent a text to The Other One.

Not her sister Jenny, who still lived with their parents in the cramped apartment with her husband and two sons, but the sister who had been sent away to live with a great-aunt. The one who still remained a mystery to the rest of the family. The one who had changed her name and preferred to communicate only by text. She called herself Elin and made her living as an author and illustrator of fantasy books, which she wrote under a pen name and no author photo. But she always managed to keep in touch sending illustrated notes to their parents and holiday cards to Rina. After Rina had returned home from the inpatient facility her sister had started to send her more notes and drawings of encouragement in an offer of friendship, which Rina eagerly accepted. So anytime Rina felt down she reached out to her as a lifeline.

Aunt Sonia and Amelia are driving me crazy!

That's nothing new. Have you told them you want to quit yet?

Yes. But Amelia's upset about it.

Too bad.

Rina sighed. She wished it were as easy as that.

I don't know what I'm doing.

That's okay. Do it anyway. Things will work out.

Rina chewed her lip and thought of telling Elin about Warren and how she was trying to help Amelia but thought better of it. Her feelings weren't something she could share with anyone.

Rina?

I'm still here.

You deserve to be happy, remember? You don't owe them anything.

It didn't feel like that.

I know. Thanks.

Although her sister's words provided some comfort, the memory of Aunt Sonia's visit still led to a sleepless night. She felt betrayed by Amelia. Why hadn't Amelia told her directly how upset she'd been about her leaving the business? Not that it would have changed Rina's mind, but they could have handled it like adults. Perhaps this was Amelia's way of getting back at her for not helping her with the special dessert. The reason didn't matter, the outcome was the same. She'd been scolded and humiliated. But she wouldn't bend.

She didn't mention Aunt Sonia's visit and Amelia had the good sense to let it go.

After another week, Rina began to put the meeting with Warren behind her. She started to feel whole again and the piercing pain and anger became a dull ache. She would survive this. She didn't care that her cousin was dating a man she'd once allowed herself to love. She would move on. Her mind was bright with ideas again.

That bright day hinted at the coming summer as she walked to her car, pleased for another successful week and thinking of a possible new item they could add to their menu before she left for good, when she heard footsteps behind her before a deep voice said, "Excuse me?"

She froze. She didn't need to turn around to know who it belonged to.

She didn't want to turn around and see his face again.

She didn't want to turn around and face her unresolved feelings for him.

But she did and her heart nearly shattered.

CHAPTER TWENTY-TWO

Recognition shone in his brown eyes.

There was nothing cold about his gaze, nothing distant about his expression, although his stance was guarded. He reminded her of the man she'd seen sitting in the bakery all those years ago. Or perhaps she was seeing what she wanted to.

She didn't know what to make of it. Had he called out to her, or had she imagined it? Perhaps he hadn't been able to get a hold of Amelia and wanted to know where she was. It was too much to hope that he'd finally remembered who she was. She took a step back and glanced at the Private Pastry Chef building. "I'm sorry. Amelia isn't here." She turned.

"I know. I—I wanted to talk to you. Do you have a minute?"

She swallowed, wishing she could get her racing heart under control. "Uh...sure."

He motioned her to a black Prius hybrid. "Let's go."

"Where?"

He unlocked the car with his key fob. "Anywhere, but here." He got inside the car, Rina hesitated a moment before she did the same. The moment she sat down she was swept away by a scent that had her thinking of sweet cherries in July and the sensation of soft sand between her toes. His scent, the scent she remembered that had taken her from the cold hospital room to a place of warmth she never wanted to leave.

"Oh, sorry about that," he said, reaching for something behind her head. She blinked. "If you move, I can get it out of your way."

She didn't know what he was talking about, so she moved to the side.

"No, that's not quite it. Do you mind?" he asked, placing a hand on her shoulder.

She shook her head.

He gently moved her forward and removed something from the back of her chair. When he tossed it in the backseat she realized she'd been leaning against his coat. For a moment she had a wild urge to grab it, put her arms inside and wrap it around her. She would inhale its scent and imagine the sweet memory of his warm body touching hers.

She turned back to the front. No, she couldn't think about that. He was Amelia's boyfriend and he wanted to talk to her. She took a deep breath and looked around the car's grey interior. The seats should have felt comfortable but she felt as if she were sitting on pins.

What could he want to talk about? Did he want more information about Amelia?

Rina waited until he turned onto the main road before she said, "If there's something you wanted to say, you can say it now."

He drove into an apartment complex and parked. "Let's walk." He got out of the car before she could protest.

What was wrong with him? What was this strange mood? She hurried up to him as he headed to the cobble path that curved through the patches of green grass and bushes of the complex. She had a strange feeling that he didn't want them to be seen together, just as he hadn't wanted it years ago. "Is something wrong?"

He shoved his hands in his dark blue trouser pockets and sighed. "I'm sorry."

"That's okay. Just tell me what you want to say."

He flashed a rueful smile. "That's it. I'm sorry."

She frowned. Did she miss something? Was there some sort of misunderstanding?

"I'm sorry I pretended not to know you," he finally said. "Thanks for following along."

Her chest tightened. So he had known, had remembered her and had ignored her on purpose. "You had your reasons."

He glanced up at the sky. "Not good ones."

"I understand. Amelia can be the jealous type and she would be annoyed that I met her prized possession, I mean, boyfriend before she did."

He flashed the same smile again, but this time it was a little sad. "Yes, you're right, but that's not the reason. It's not a reason I'm proud of."

"You don't have to explain." She didn't want to know.

She could guess the reason. He didn't want to admit that he'd known someone like her. He was successful now, more than she was, they were on different levels. "You've done so much and she doesn't have to know that—"

Warren stopped walking and looked at her. His gaze intense. The same intense gaze from all those years ago when she'd fallen in love with him because he didn't make her feel invisible. That she was truly flesh and blood; that she mattered. "You saved my life."

Rina shook her head, fighting back tears. She didn't want to feel this way about him. She didn't want him to be grateful for something anyone would have done. "No, you did it."

"If you hadn't taken the time to tell me what I didn't want to hear, I might not be here right now. You gave me strength I'd lost. I'd stopped believing in myself, but for some reason you believed in me without judgment. I've never forgotten that. Part of me is thankful, but part of me hates the debt I owe you."

Rina shook her head, shaken by the passion in his voice. "There's no debt. It was a gift. You can live your life now."

"Few people know about my past."

"I won't say anything. You have my word."

She saw the tenseness of his posture ease. "Thanks."

"But don't be ashamed of it either. You overcame a lot. You're an admirable man."

He suddenly laughed and the sound was genuine and fresh. "I should have known. The moment I first took a bite of Amelia's croissant there was something familiar about it. An indescribable feeling. It must run in the family, the generosity and kindness you share. I'm lucky to have met you both."

Rina felt her heart painfully constrict. She didn't want to feel anything for him, but she felt even more than she had only a few weeks ago because he was even better than she'd remembered. She would continue to love him, she couldn't seem to stop herself, but from a distance no matter how close they were. She'd never reveal her feelings. They would be a secret. "Hmm."

"I still owe you lunch."

"Another time."

"So I'm not forgiven yet?"

"You're forgiven, I just have something I have to get back to. Tell Amelia we can do it another time."

"Is that a promise?"

She hoped he was being polite and would forget the offer. "It is."

If only she could tell her heart to stop beating so fast, if only she would stop wanting to lean in closer to him, to inhale his scent, even hearing him breathe gave her a certain thrill. But it was not to be. He loved her cousin, her cousin loved him.

"So how are you doing?"

Rina paused. The question surprised her. She thought their conversation was over, had come to its natural conclusion, but here he was with those kind brown eyes of his asking her how she was and meaning it. She wasn't used to that. She swallowed and continued walking again. "I'm fine."

"What are you doing? Amelia didn't tell me the specifics. Only that you work together."

"That's right...I do a lot of administrative and managerial things for her."

"So she can focus on the baking."

"Yes, something like that."

"That sounds about right. You seem like the kind of person who would pay attention to detail, while Amelia would want to be free to focus on the art needed in the kitchen."

Rina wanted to tell him that baking was also very detail-oriented but knew that wasn't the time, she was already lying to him. There was no need to reveal that truth.

"Do you like it?" he asked.

She frowned. "Like it?"

"Yes, what you do."

"Why?"

He shrugged. "Just curious. I wouldn't have thought administrative tasks were your thing."

She sniffed. "You don't know me."

He sent her a significant look. "I know you enough."

That was true. Somehow in that alleyway all those years ago, staring down each other's secrets, they'd gone beyond being strangers.

She bit her lip. "You're right. It's not really, but..." She let her words die away.

He nudged her with his arm when she stopped. "But what?"

"I'll be doing something else soon. I hope. I don't really know what. A-Amelia hired...uh...someone else, I've trained them."

"So what will you do now?"

"I don't know."

He was quiet a moment before he said, "Is Rina short for Irene?"

"No, it's Cirina, but nobody calls me that."

"Good, then I'll call you that from now on."

"Why?"

"Because I think it suits you."

The thought gave her a tiny thrill.

"Amelia told me you like to cook."

Rina stared at him surprised. "She did?"

"Yes," Warren said with a laugh. "Don't look so surprised. It's not supposed to be a secret, is it?"

"No, but I didn't think she'd tell you that about me."

He held up his forefinger and his thumb as though measuring a small object. "Well, you also gave me a tiny clue."

"I did?"

He nodded. "The white chef's jacket you were wearing when I came by."

Right. Of course. She'd forgotten about that. "Hmm."

"Is cooking another trait that runs in the family?"

"I have my own interest in food," Rina said, trying to sound as vague as possible.

"Actually, I could use your help."

She pointed to herself. "My help?"

He nodded. "My private chef just quit and I've been living on takeaways and it's starting to get to me. I pay well and I'm not particular. However, I don't eat anything with a face except on weekends."

"I'm not sure—"

"If you say yes, I'll tell Amelia so that everything's

above board. I've asked her twice for a recommendation and she keeps forgetting."

Rina sighed, that sounded like her cousin. If it didn't directly impact her she tended to let things slip her mind.

"I need a cook and you need a job. I think it's perfect." He pressed his hands together. "Please."

"But I—"

"Two weeks, if you hate it that much I won't stop you from quitting. Plus...you know your cousin can be a little...possessive?"

"Yes," Rina said cautious, wondering where he was headed.

"I've had problems before with my staff. This is a secret between us. You cannot tell her what I'm about to tell you."

"Okay."

"Umm...a few times I've had...staff trying to have more than a professional relationship with me, if you get my meaning."

"Uh...huh."

"Once I found my housekeeper in my bed. Naked only holding a feather duster."

Rina started to laugh.

Warren didn't smile. "I'm not joking."

Rina covered her mouth and tried to suppress a giggle. "I'm sorry."

"There was the groundskeeper who kept working with his shirt off, I thought he was hot so I gave him a glass of water. He took the glass from me and told me he knew a better way I could help him cool down."

Rina bit her lip.

"And there was the dog walker."

"You have a dog?"

"No, but she did. She told me that one of her charges had somehow gotten loose in my yard. I have a couple acres so it's possible. I tried to help her so I let her inside and—"

"She tried to wrap a collar around you and told you to be a 'good boy'."

He frowned. "It's not funny."

Rina smiled. "Yes, it is."

The corner of his mouth kicked up in a quick grin. "I guess it is a little. As you can guess there was no dog to find."

Rina widened her eyes in fake amazement. "Imagine that."

"But that's not why I need your help. My last chef was the worst. She..." He briefly closed his eyes. "Her cooking was divine. What she could do with yellow rice was amazing. I told her so." He opened his eyes and sighed. "I complimented her every chance I could, perhaps too much because she got the wrong impression."

"So one day you found her naked on the kitchen island with a rose between her teeth."

He stared at her amazed. "You were there?"

Her brows shot up. "That really happened?"

Warren laughed. "No, of course not."

She playfully punched him in the arm then stared up at him alarmed. Knowing his past she shouldn't have touched him like that even in fun. "I'm sorry. I shouldn't have done that."

His expression turned dark. He rubbed the spot

where she'd struck him and said in a low voice, "No, you shouldn't have. Especially knowing what I went through."

She took a step back, but before she could apologize again his face split into a wide grin. He winked. "Relax. It's okay. It's behind me now. I know you'd never hurt me."

She released a breath and took another step back. His smile fell. "I really scared you, didn't I?"

She nodded.

"I'm sorry. I couldn't resist. Teasing you is fun."

She folded her arms and started walking back to the car. "You should warn me next time."

"That would defeat the purpose. Hold on." He grabbed her arm, forcing her to a halt. He rolled up his sleeve and showed her his bicep, flexing the muscle. "See? Not even a bruise."

But she wasn't looking for a bruise as she let her eyes linger over the slope of his muscle, the shape of his shoulders, the size of his hand. He was beautifully made. She finally lifted her gaze to his eyes and saw him watching her with amusement. Her face burned with embarrassment. She turned and continued walking. "You're a flirt. I bet you led your staff on."

He held up his hands. "I swear I didn't. I'm innocent."

"I don't believe you."

"The wedding cake wasn't my fault."

She frowned at him. "What?"

"You heard me."

"She baked you a wedding cake?"

He shook his head. "No, she had it delivered. She hosted a surprise wedding. She thought I was in love with her and was too shy to tell her. She invited her family and friends. To say the least, things didn't end well."

"You had to tell her the truth in front of all those people?"

"No, I married her knowing it wasn't really legal. I didn't sign any papers, gave a fake middle name and waited until the ceremony was over."

Rina stared at him, unsure.

He placed a hand over his heart. "I'm not kidding. I need your help. I haven't had much success with household staff and part of me wonders if Amelia is having a hard time helping me with my chef request because I've told her some of my stories."

"I thought you wanted to keep this a secret."

"I do. I wasn't as specific with her as I was with you. I told her that the housekeeper tried to hug me and the groundskeeper winked. I didn't tell her that twice his hand brushed against my butt."

"You didn't tell me that either."

He hesitated. "Oh. Right. Never mind."

"I get the picture."

"He still comes by sometimes. Gives good suggestions."

"You don't have to explain."

"I didn't tell her about the others."

"The dog walker and the private chef?"

He cleared his throat. "And the contractor and event planner," he waved his hand before she could speak, "but we don't need to get into that. My point is she may be uncomfortable. However, if you worked for me she wouldn't be because there's no chance of you being interested in me or vice versa."

No chance. No chance. No chance. The words seemed to echo in Rina's mind, as a tiny pain seared her heart. As she'd feared Warren didn't see her as a woman. She was just a safe nonentity to cook his meals and keep his girlfriend happy. How stupid of her to actually think he'd been flirting, he'd merely been teasing her as if she were an amusing child or cute puppy.

He was right. Amelia wouldn't mind and Rina didn't have a set plan for the future. She didn't know what she wanted to do next. This opportunity could give her a chance to think about her next strategy, but she still had to be careful. She felt more for him than she should.

"I have to talk to Amelia first."

He nodded pleased, his words almost as soft as a caress. "Thanks for helping me, Cirina. It will be a pleasure working with you."

"You don't know if she'll agree, yet."

Warren sent her a look, a slow, sly grin touching his lips that made it clear that he'd become a man used to getting his way.

CHAPTER TWENTY-THREE

"That's a great idea!" Amelia said when Rina called her that evening. "You could find out even more about him for me."

Rina felt like falling face first into her couch, but resisted the urge and continued to walk back and forth in her living room. "I'll just be cooking some meals, not going through his closet and drawers."

"But you could," Amelia said with increased enthusiasm.

"You've been dating him for months I'm sure you know plenty about him."

"Not as much as you think," she grumbled.

"I'm not going to spy on him. This will be temporary. I'm thinking two months."

"Six."

"Three."

Rina knew Amelia was trying to extend their original six month agreement, but didn't feel like arguing. "Fine."

She sat on the couch and stared up at the ceiling, wondering if she was really doing the right thing. "By then you should have learned enough to start baking for him yourself."

"I quit the class."

She sat up. "You what?"

"It was getting too hard. Besides I think I've gotten a lot better. You'll see."

"Can you make sugar cookies without burning them?"

"Almost."

"Almost?"

"The last time I got distracted otherwise they would have been perfect."

Rina rubbed her forehead. "That's the point, when baking you can't be distracted. Everything has to be—"

"I know, I know pay attention to detail," Amelia said impatient. "So you'll do it, right? You have to. I need you to take the job and watch whoever comes sniffing around him. You'll be my eyes and ears."

"You might as well tag him."

"Trust me I tried, but he wouldn't accept the watch I gave him. It has top level surveillance capabilities."

Rina began to laugh before she realized her cousin was serious. "I'm certain you don't have to go that far. He's someone you can trust."

"Trusting isn't easy."

"He's not Gerry." Gerry had cheated on her more than once. Rina could understand her cousin's vigilance even if it was a little misguided.

"So you'll do it for me?"

"Sure." But also for herself. She'd get to cook for Warren, be by his side even briefly before he was torn from her forever.

❦

I'LL DO IT.

Warren stared at the text message Cirina had sent him and smiled.

He really shouldn't feel this relieved and happy but he was. He couldn't wait to find out what Cirina would prepare for him.

Plus he felt as if he'd been given a chance to help her as she'd once helped him.

His life had turned out better than he could have imagined. Leaving his wife hadn't been easy. He'd had to swallow his pride and ask for his brother's help so he could have a place to stay while he got his life back on track. But he'd managed to slowly regain his confidence and after helping a friend with the score for an indie game he'd developed, Warren had found his calling. He'd loved video games since childhood, although rarely had the time to indulge, only getting a chance on the occasion he visited with his cousins and watch from a distance. In his later years, when he'd broken free from his family's hold, he'd played video games as often as he could (to his wife's annoyance) and been impressed by the music of the different genres.

He admired the work of top video game composer Nobuo Uematsu. As his new career slowly took hold he used his orchestral background to compose sweeping scores for cinematic, larger-than-life games and also blended his classical training with electronics for more action focused games. Soon he wasn't only composing scores but also helping with sound design.

Four years ago he'd founded his production company Five High LLC, which developed multiple audio products and services for videos games. The company expanded his role from composer to project manager, voice directing and consulting. It was very successful.

Not that his parents were impressed. When he'd first told them his goal they had been repulsed. "Imagine a gourmet chef using their talents at a fast food franchise," his mother had said. "It's a passing phase," his father had said.

They were both wrong, but he didn't care. He loved what he did. He created the music he wanted, the way he wanted to, he also worked with other creative people—musicians, producers, audio directors—who stimulated him. He lived life on his terms and now he also had an amazing woman to share it with.

He still felt guilty for pretending not to know Cirina when they'd met. But he had too much to lose. With one word she could have toppled the image he'd constructed of himself. She could reveal the man beneath the years of strategic planning, counseling and sacrifice.

He was so close to having all that he wanted. With one look, she could destroy it and it angered him that he stood at her mercy. That day he'd felt every nerve ending come to life as he stared at her, silently begging her not to hint at knowing him. Every time Amelia touched him he felt as if his skin was on fire. He wanted to run. But he didn't move, he played the role of successful boyfriend meeting his girlfriend's relative for the first time. He'd grown adept at playacting, his life before now had trained him well.

It had taken him weeks to try to figure out what to do. He waited to see if Amelia would mention anything about the meeting that would reveal that Rina and he had a history. But nothing came and his fears subsided. His secret was safe.

Soon anger and fear turned into guilt and finally regret. Cirina had given him so much. He shouldn't have treated her that way. Even worse, he worried about her. As much as she was polite and smiled, there was a light missing from her eyes. She didn't look happy and she didn't look well. She was still too thin, although not as bad as the past, and there was a strange hunger he couldn't quite place. She'd once saved him. He planned to do the same for her.

"Abort mission. Abort mission!"

The loud whirring sound jerked him out of his thoughts. He refocused on one of the three screens in front of him. Warren yanked off his headphones and frowned at his friend Steve Adeji.

Steve frowned back and at over six feet, dark as cobalt and made of pure muscle he did the expression well. He owned a business that designed video games, after disappointing his parents by not becoming the aerospace engineer they'd expected him to be, Warren had invited him over to listen to his latest score.

"Have you decided to revisit Earth?" Steve said.

Warren shifted his gaze back at the screen where his composition was displayed. "What don't you like?"

"I said that the pacing's off."

"Oh sorry."

"About five hundred times."

Warren couldn't help a laugh. "No need to exaggerate."

"What's up?"

"Nothing."

"That must mean Amelia."

"No, actually...I hired a new chef."

"Female?"

He nodded.

Steve gave a low whistle. "You're a brave man. It was nice knowing you."

"No. It will be fine this time. She's Amelia's cousin and I—" Warren stopped before he mentioned that he'd met her before. There was no reason for him to know that. "I trust her."

"Amelia's cousin and she's okay with that? Is this woman ninety years old or something?"

"A little younger than me I think."

"Then she must be ugly."

"She's not ugly."

"There is *no way* Amelia would have a young woman cooking in your kitchen unless she was ugly."

Warren felt his temper pricked. "I met her. She's not ugly. She's just...different."

"Different how?"

"I don't want to talk about it."

Steve flashed a knowing grin. "Just think about her?"

Warren shook his head. "I'm just relieved. Amelia's the woman for me." Before Steve could ask any questions he picked up his headphones and said, "Let's see how I can adjust the pace."

CHAPTER TWENTY-FOUR

Cooking was different than baking. Rina took a deep breath and repeated the statement almost as a mantra as she whipped up cranberry muffins in her kitchen that Saturday.

Cooking wasn't as intimate for her, it didn't have the same history, memory, sensations, it would be okay. Making that distinction would help her keep her feelings in check.

Working for Warren was a chance to refocus and start fresh. So she'd be in his house, it wasn't like she was living there. She'd prepare his meals; leave some heating instructions then leave. How hard could that be? She would have to brush up on some skills that she'd let lapse, but that wouldn't be difficult either.

She would prepare the menu as well and since he wasn't particular she wouldn't have to be stressed about it. Cooking didn't have to be as precise, it could be more of a fun chemistry experiment—an extra dash of something here or there wouldn't overwhelm the taste or texture if she handled it right.

She placed the muffins in the oven and told herself she'd made the right choice. That it would help her get over him.

But she still couldn't sleep that night. She still couldn't stop herself from imaging what his kitchen looked like. Country cozy or modern? She hoped he had been telling her the truth about his tastes, some people said they weren't particular about things, but really were. If he was, she'd quit and do something else. That was the freedom. She could walk away; she didn't have to do this.

The problem was she wanted to.

Even more so when she finally walked into his kitchen that Monday. The moment she entered, Rina immediately got a sense that something was wrong. The kitchen was beautifully put together with granite counter tops, but she had a terrible feeling about it and she didn't know why. It was clean. Somehow too clean.

"If there's anything you need," Warren said with a wide sweep of his hand. "Just let me know." His cell phone rang. He looked at it before he said, "Sorry, I have to get this. I'll be right back."

Rina watched him leave before she released a sigh of relief. She'd have to grow accustomed to having him in her space, but she hadn't yet and she really liked to be alone to get acquainted with the environment she was supposed to work in. However, the moment she'd arrived he hadn't left her side.

He'd barely given her a chance to take in the house's sweeping curved driveway, the steps leading up to the arched entryway and the sleek wooden accents of the corridor before he motioned to the garden and conservatory where she could rest as if she were there as a guest instead of as a worker. She'd found his attention amusing and could see how his generosity could be misinterpreted or exploited.

But now she was free to look around without him.

Her gaze went to the stove, an induction cooktop with solid fixtures, then it shifted to the black stainless steel French door refrigerator. She walked over to the cupboards, bent down and opened it.

Her heart fell. She briefly closed her eyes and softly swore.

It explained a lot. She opened a few more cupboards and her mood continued to plummet until she didn't think it was possible to descend any further.

She opened the fridge and the sight inside explained everything she needed to know, but didn't make the situation any easier to face. How was she supposed to tell him? What was she supposed to do? He'd seemed so proud to show her what he had. It was going to hurt him and that was the last thing she wanted.

When she heard his footsteps returning she quickly closed the fridge, all the cupboards and prepared to face him.

He smiled at her. "Sorry, about that. So, is everything in order?"

She shook her head.

His smile fell. "I know it's not state of the art."

"That's not it," she said quickly, not wanting him to

feel uncomfortable. "I may have doubted your story about the chef before, but I don't now."

"What do you mean?"

"Since you've been eating out a lot you wouldn't have noticed, but..." She opened a cupboard. "There are no pots, no pans, barely any cutlery." She opened a few more. "There's almost nothing here to cook with."

Warren stared at the empty shelves shocked.

"It seems she didn't take your rejection very well."

He swore.

"I'm sorry."

"I can't believe this." He pointed at her. "Amelia can never know about this." He walked up to the cupboard and closed it.

"Too late. I already told her."

He spun around his eyes wide. "What?"

Rina nodded, solemn. "Yes, while you were on the phone I called her and told her and even sent a video."

He frowned, realizing she was teasing him. "Don't do that."

"Then give me some credit. Of course I won't tell her. Why would I?"

He held up his hand. "Fine, we're even." He narrowed his eyes, with the hint of a smile. "You've got a mean streak."

She motioned to the cupboards. "Not as mean as this."

He rubbed the back of his neck. "You're right. This is embarrassing." Warren leaned his head back and groaned. "She got me."

"She got your pots. Unless she plans to get intimate

with them in ways I don't want to imagine, I would hardly call that a victory."

He grinned. "Well, when you put it like that, I guess you have a point."

"She just proved you were right and to be grateful she's out of your life."

His grin widened. "And I get to hire you instead."

She wished his grin didn't make her heart do back flips. "Right." She looked away from him, determined to focus on the kitchen. "This is easy to fix. I can't cook anything yet, but in the interim I can bring over—"

"No, it's okay. I'll pay. Buy whatever you need and I'll reimburse you." He pulled out his wallet. "Better yet charge it."

She glanced at the credit card. "What's your budget?"

He frowned. "Budget?"

"Yes, your limit."

"Do you need one?"

She sighed. "If I spent ten thousand dollars you'd be fine with that?"

He shrugged.

"You're too nice."

He folded his arms. "Of course I would expect every meal to be the level of a gourmet restaurant, cooked to perfection each and every time, no recipe repeated—*ever*—sautéed, grilled and baked to a level of craftsmanship that would make it all worth it. And if you failed to meet that standard I'd remind you what each pot cost line item by line item." He winked. "I'm nice but I'm not *that* nice."

Rina laughed. "That's good to know."

"Whatever you need."

"Within reason."

He nodded.

"With a chip installed so that they can never been stolen again."

He shook his head. "No, this time I'd find you and make you pay."

She shrugged. "So what? You don't scare me."

"I'd send Amelia first."

Rina shivered. "You win."

Warren laughed. "Good."

She liked his smile, his laughter, the light in his eyes. That wasn't good. She took his card and cleared her throat. "I'll make a list."

CHAPTER TWENTY-FIVE

*I*t was almost too easy.

Rina stood at the counter kitchen with Warren and finalized the next week's menu. After three weeks this had become a tradition.

Warren had a simple routine: Breakfast at 8:30, lunch at 2, dinner at 7, although he'd warned her that when he worked on a major project or had a tight deadline those times would change, and he was truly not fussy with the suggestions she made. She knew she was fortunate because she'd heard from other private chefs stories about how some clients changed their minds and wanted to be told every day what the menu would be, adjusting it to suit their whims. Warren didn't care as long as it was on time, to his specifications and tasted good.

She was about to have him approve the menu, wishing he didn't have to stand so close when he was looking at it, wishing he didn't have to smell so good, when the doorbell rang.

Warren glanced at his watch. "Oh, that's right. I forgot Peter was dropping by."

Rina made a groan of annoyance. She wished she could have been prepared. "I'll put together some refreshments."

"Great. Thanks." He left the kitchen.

Rina quickly set out almonds, cut apples and pears she'd prepared for another dish before she cut a Camembert cheese into thin slices. Peter. Why did that name sound familiar? Didn't he have a brother named Peter?

She nearly dropped the knife as an awful realization overtook her.

His brother! The one married to her former boss at the Bee Sweet bakery! Peter knew she was a trained pastry chef. That would ruin everything. He couldn't see her.

She quickly searched the kitchen for a place to hide as she heard the hum of their voices and the click of their footsteps approach. She dove into the pantry just in time.

"That's strange," she heard Warren say. "She was just here."

"Looks good anyway," she heard Peter say. She imagined him going to the platter and taking a bite of a sliced apple topped with cheese.

"Her food is amazing."

"So you've said. Julian is still interested in talking to Amelia about her business. He could use some ideas."

Rina gasped. Peter was *still* with him?

"Did you hear that?" Warren asked.

Rina covered her mouth and squeezed her eyes shut certain they could hear her heart pounding.

"No, I didn't," Peter said. "You're avoiding the subject again."

"I'm not avoiding anything. I just don't know if Amelia can help him."

"You don't know that."

"I'll ask her again, but I won't make any promises. She's very busy."

"And she's fine with her cousin working for you?"

"She's perfectly safe. When you meet her you'll understand."

Rina prayed that wouldn't happen. But she couldn't hide in the pantry forever. How long were they going to stand there? How could she avoid Peter? Should she avoid him? Maybe he wouldn't remember her, their meetings had been brief.

"I'm happy for you," Peter said, "but you still have to be careful. A woman like Amelia—"

Warren sighed. "Not this again."

"Listen, you nearly—"

"It's the past. I'm a different man now. Amelia is nothing like...I love her."

"Isn't that sudden?"

"I've never been so certain and if you tasted her food you'd know why."

"What does that have to do with anything?"

"A lot. More than you know." He lowered his voice. "She made me Jamaican sweet potato pudding."

"Truly?" Peter asked with a note of awe.

"Truly."

"And you didn't leave me any?"

"Mi sorry," Warren said not sounding sorry at all. "I

took one bite and couldn't stop myself. But I thought of you fondly when I finished every bite of her coconut cake."

"Shut up you greedy bastard," Peter said without malice.

Warren laughed. "Now you see what I mean. She's beautiful both inside and out. She really cares about me, I can literally taste it. I know at first she can seem—"

"Vain, flighty, self-centered?"

"Yes, but there's more to her. She's smart, her business is proof of that, and she's generous, plus she has a good heart. The desserts she's made for me take a lot of time and she's always eager to make sure I like them. I know it sounds strange, but she reveals herself in her food. She's...I've never felt this way before."

"Okay," Peter said resigned. "I don't have much time to wait. I have an appointment cross town. I thought you wanted me to meet Cirina."

"I wonder if she went out back. Let me go look for her."

"Don't bother. I'll meet her another time."

Rina waited to hear their voices fade down the hall before she emerged from her hiding place.

Her heart continued to pound, but not due to the fear of being discovered. But because of Warren's words.

He loved Amelia.

It didn't matter how close he stood next to her, how easily he smiled at her, how much he complimented her and made her feel good. She was just an employee. Amelia's cousin—nothing more.

It was the way it should be.

It shouldn't hurt this much.

She knew the strength of his feelings for her cousin but to hear him say the words made her longing feel dirty. Of course he loved Amelia. There was no reason not to. She was beautiful, smart and did have a good heart.

She briefly covered her eyes. She was supposed to be trying to get over him. Not falling for him even harder.

"There you are!"

She jumped and her hand fell from her eyes.

"Where did you disappear to?" Warren said, closing the distance between them, a puzzled look on his face.

"I...uh...thought you'd want privacy."

He picked up an apple slice and took a bite. "I would have told you if I did. I'd wanted to introduce you."

"You didn't say so."

"You're right. Next time, stick around."

She licked her lip, hesitant. "Actually, I'd prefer not to meet anyone."

"What?"

"I don't like feeling on display. There's no reason for me to meet your family."

He frowned. "I'm proud of you. I didn't think... I'm sorry you'd think I was trying to show you off."

"I work for you. No one else needs to know about me. Okay? Otherwise I can't work here." She picked up the menu. "Now I need to do some shopping. Excuse me."

CHAPTER TWENTY-SIX

Steven stared at him. "She stole your pots?"

Warren nodded. It had been a month since Cirina had started working for him and he felt comfortable mentioning what had really happened, although the fact that she didn't want to meet anyone still bothered him. They both sat in Steve's living room in front of his large flat screen with a video game ready to start, but Warren's casual comment about his former chef had stopped Steve from beginning.

He set down his console and turned fully to him. "For real? You're not making this up?"

"Why would I make this up? The surprise wedding freaked me out enough."

"True."

"I'm lucky she didn't steal the stove. She basically took everything she could carry. She left me some glasses and dishes though. I guess that's something."

Steve picked up his console. "She probably didn't have enough time."

"I'd like to think that she was being considerate."

"Or she knew you wouldn't notice so she would get away with it longer than she would have."

"Maybe."

"So what are you going to do?"

"Cirina's already in charge."

"Cirina?"

He nodded. "Yes, my new chef. She took care of it. And the meals have been amazing." He held up his hand. "And don't worry, I told you, she's different. I can trust her."

"But you won't let me meet her."

"Not yet."

"Afraid I'll steal her away?"

"Maybe." Plus she doesn't like meeting strangers.

Steve rested a hand on his chest. "I'm wounded."

"Find a band aid."

"Does Amelia know?"

He sent his friend a significant look. "There's nothing for her to know."

Steve nodded taking the hint and started the game.

But Steve didn't like waiting. He *had* to meet Warren's new chef. He drove to his place at a time when he knew Warren wouldn't be home. He'd texted Warren twice to make sure the event he was attending was still on. He had to meet this woman his friend was talking about. The one that Amelia didn't feel threatened by. His friend didn't have the greatest of taste in women and he was too curious to let it slide.

He knocked on the door and waited. Maybe she wouldn't open it. Since she didn't live there that was a possibility. He started to turn when the front door opened. "Warren isn't here," a woman said.

Steve was rarely speechless, especially in the presence of a woman. He was usually at his best then, but this woman left him tongue-tied. She was nothing like he expected. Strikingly attractive, but understated, smaller than he'd imagined, thin, almost fragile looking, but her eyes showed a strength that humbled him. No excited him. She was fierce. He liked his women fierce. If he had a particular type, she would be it.

"...but if you wish to leave a message at the beep."

Damn, she was funny too. He swallowed. He'd better say something before she closed the door in his face.

"I had to see you," he said in a rush but when she looked stunned and a little wary, he realized his mistake. Damn. What was wrong with him? "I mean...I—I...Uh are you Cirina?"

"No, I'm Rina."

"Oh, I thought—"

She folded her arms. "That we were friends and that you had the right to call me by my given name?"

He felt properly scolded. "No."

"What do you want?"

"Oh...I uh...I came to see you."

Her eyes narrowed. "Why?"

How could suspicion look so sexy? "I'm a friend of Warren's. If you'd let me come in—"

She flashed a superior smile that affected him more than he wanted it to. "Nice try. That's not going to work. I don't know who you are and unless Warren tells me he's expecting a guest, you're going to have to talk to him directly."

"No," he said in a near panic. The last thing he wanted was for Warren to know he was there. "I was never here." He waved his hand and took a quick step back, forgetting that he was on the top step, he lost his balance and stumbled back, he twisted himself before he hit the ground, skinning his palm. The impact hurt, his pride hurt even more.

She rushed over to him. "Are you alright?"

"I'm fine," he grumbled, rising to his feet.

She grabbed his wrist, staring at his cut palm and the blood that seeped from it. "You're not fine. This needs to be cleaned. If you hadn't looked so clumsy, I'd think you'd done this on purpose. I know you didn't," she said when he opened his mouth. "I think you would have found a less painful way to get inside. Let me just call Warren and—"

"No," Steve said. He tried to jerk his hand away from her, but her grip was strong and all he managed to do was pull her closer and he got a whiff of lemon and vanilla.

"Why not?"

"I wasn't supposed to come. He can't know I'm here."

"You're not a friend of his?" She looked him up and down with new interest. "Oh, I see. Were you the groundskeeper?"

He frowned insulted. Did he look like a laborer? "Groundskeeper? What? No! I'm a game designer."

"Board games?"

Was she kidding? He wasn't sure. "No, video games."

"I see." She didn't look like she believed him. "If you came to check out the competition—" She sighed. "Never mind. How you feel about Warren is none of my business."

"What?"

"And I'm sorry to disappoint you. Amelia isn't here either. But that's not important. We really need to get this cleaned, so as much as I hate to say it, come in." She sighed and dragged him inside.

CHAPTER TWENTY-SEVEN

*W*hat a strange man, Rina thought as she cleaned up his wound in the upstairs bathroom, which was big enough for both of them (he made the powder room on the lower level feel as small as a broom closet). When she'd opened the door, he could barely stop staring at her, she had yet to understand what he found so strange about her, and now as she wrapped his wound in a bandage, he could barely look at her. She could tell he was embarrassed, but she preferred it that way. It helped to subdue his intense energy. He was like a whirlwind, but falling and hurting his hand had calmed him. She'd only managed to learn his name was "Steve" and nothing more.

"I know one-sided love is difficult," Rina said, trying to sound understanding, "but I think it's better to save a friendship, don't you?"

"Hmm."

"Unless it hurts too much and then it's better to keep your distance."

He seemed so miserable that she felt a little sorry for him. "Would you like—" She stopped when she heard the front door close. "Oh, he's home early."

Steve's eyes grew wide. He jumped up and dashed into the shower and closed the curtain.

She pulled it back. "What are you doing?"

"I've gotta hide. He can't see me."

"Well, you can't hide in there. One of the first things he likes to do is have a shower." She grabbed the back of his shirt. "And no, you're not crawling out the window either. You're too big anyway." She held up her hand. "Stay here and let me see where he is."

He nodded.

She peeked into the corridor and saw that it was empty and waved him forward. They hurried to the top of the stairs then she saw Warren and pushed Steve back.

"There you are," Warren said heading towards her.

She launched at him, something she'd never done and said, "You look famished. Let me go make you something."

"Sounds great, let me freshen up first."

"You can freshen up later." She pulled him to the kitchen, glancing at Steve as he held his breath.

Moments later Warren sat in the kitchen and ate the crackers with pesto Rina had prepared for him. "These are delicious."

She watched Steve silently creep past the kitchen entrance and held her breath. Just a few yards and he'd be safe.

"Is he still trying to leave without me knowing?" Warren said.

Steve paused with one foot in the air.

Warren didn't turn as he picked up another cracker.

Rina cleared her throat. "I don't know—"

"I might not have known someone was here if I hadn't seen a particular person's bright orange Subaru parked out front."

Steve closed his eyes.

"So he might as well sit down and tell me what he's been up to."

Steve hesitated. Rina motioned him forward. He sat down with reluctance. He reached for a cracker. Warren slapped his hand away. "I said you could sit. I didn't say you could eat. Start talking."

"You wouldn't let me meet her," Steve said sounding like a petulant child.

Rina motioned to the exit, feeling uncomfortable. "Let me leave you two alone."

Warren nodded. "That's a good idea. I'll talk to you later about what you two were doing upstairs."

"It was nothing," Rina said, shocked by the implication.

"I told her I didn't want to," Steve said.

"So she dragged you by force. All eighty-five pounds of her."

Rina folded her arms. "Hey!"

"She's stronger than she looks."

Warren motioned Rina away when she opened her mouth. "We'll talk at dinner." He shook his head when she continued to try to speak. "Only then."

She sighed, sent Steve a look that said you'd-better-fix this, before she left.

Warren rested his chin in his hand and fluttered his eyelashes. "Alone at last."

"I'm sorry."

"What did you do?"

"Nothing. I only wanted to meet her and...it got a little complicated."

"Did she attack you?"

"What? No."

Warren nodded to his friend's bandaged hand. "Then what happened?"

"I tripped...she wasn't what I'd expected, I got clumsy. It wasn't on purpose. I swear. She offered to clean it up."

"And you went willingly."

"I didn't want to be rude. Plus it hurt like hell."

"Did she kiss it and make it feel all better?"

Steve frowned. "Shut up."

Warren nodded. "What do you think?"

"I made a mistake. I'm sorry."

"No, about her. Now that you've met her has your curiosity been satisfied?"

Steve reached for a cracker again. "Very."

Warren moved the plate out of reach. "I'm surprised she opened the door. She doesn't like strangers."

Steve stood and reached over to grab one. "Is she seeing anyone?"

Warren slapped his hand away. "Keep your hands off my chef."

"Sharing is caring. Didn't they teach you that in kindergarten?"

"I'm not sharing her with you."

"You can't stop me."

Warren met his gaze and lowered his voice. "I know things about you you wouldn't want me to share."

Steve sat back in his seat. "I could say the same." He narrowed his eyes. "Are you sure Amelia shouldn't be jealous?"

"I love Amelia. I like Cirina. I respect her. Unfortunately, I know you too well. She can do better."

"Ouch."

"You know it too."

Steven leaned forward and slowly pulled the plate towards him. "But she looks interesting."

Warren let him take the plate and smiled when his friend took a bite. "She is interesting, but you always get bored."

"This is really good."

"It's the tip of the iceberg."

"Invite me for dinner."

"No."

"When can I try her cooking?"

"Someday."

"You're stalling."

"Of course I am. Once you taste her cooking it won't be enough. You'll want more. You'll want another creamy scalloped potato arrangement for dinner; frittata for lunch and a soft strawberry crepe for breakfast."

"She uses berries?"

"Fresh," Warren said with emphasis.

"What's her rate?"

"Go home."

Steve stood. "Amelia's blind."

"What do you mean?"

"Rina may not be a conventional beauty, but she's..." He winked. "I don't blame you for wanting to keep her for yourself."

Warren frowned. "I told you—"

Steve held up his hands. "I know. But the strange thing is it could be between you two."

Warren remained in the kitchen after his friend left. He stared at the empty plate his mind spinning. His friend's words shook him. How could he even imagine that he could be with Cirina. Of course it couldn't be. Never. They were friends. She knew about his past. There was no way she'd see him in another light, not that he wanted her to. Things were perfect as they were.

But Steve's reaction had him thinking about Cirina in a different way. He'd never really seen her as a woman before. He knew she was in a vague sort of way, but not in any way that had interested him. She had a nice face, far from beautiful, her mouth turned down at the corners, her eyes were too sharp, her features angular rather than smooth. If she had a figure, he didn't know it. She was slender on the verge of skinny and yet...

And yet he found her charming. Lovely in an under-stated way. If Steve was really interested in her, who was he to stand in the way? She was a grown woman and Steve a good looking successful guy. Cirina could do worse.

But despite all the logic, Warren resisted the idea. He

wanted someone different for her, he sensed a vulnerability she was careful to hide. He wanted to protect her from his friend's casual interest. He didn't know much about her, except that he sensed she'd suffered heartbreak in the past. She needed someone she could trust.

Someone like him.

Of course, it couldn't be *him* since he was with Amelia, but someone similar. Someone who would be patient, tender with her. Someone...

Warren pushed himself from the table and swore. Why the hell was he thinking about her at all? It was Steve's fault. He'd filled his head with nonsense. Cirina's private life, especially her private pain, was none of his business.

He jumped when he felt a soft hand on his shoulder. He spun around.

"I said your name," Rina said. "But you didn't hear me."

"What are you still doing here?" he said with more force than he'd meant to.

"I couldn't wait until dinner to talk to you. I wasn't eavesdropping, I waited outside until I saw Steve leave. I hope you aren't too angry."

He ran a hand down his face. "I'm furious that you—"

"I told him to leave, but then he got hurt and I couldn't just let him bleed." She held up her hand. "And before you say anything, I hope you weren't too harsh with him. People can't help how they feel and sometimes they'll do impulsive things."

Warren frowned. "He knows exactly how I feel."

"But the heart cannot help where it leads you."

"I don't want to talk about it. Just be careful of him."

"He cares about you. I don't think he stole anything. I watched him closely."

Why would he steal anything? It didn't matter, she was clearly rattled by the event and it made him feel guilty. "This is none of my business, but I'm going to ask anyway, are you seeing anyone?"

She stiffened. "I don't need a therapist."

"No, wait." He shook his head. "Sorry, that came out wrong. Never mind. It doesn't matter. I'm sorry he bothered you."

"It's okay. He seemed sweet, sort of shy."

Warren laughed. "Shy?"

"Yes, so I hope you can still work together." Before he could reply she said, "And now I'll go shopping to get the items for dinner."

Thankfully, she was able to get over the strange events of the afternoon and prepared a meal that Warren praised. However, it was as she was cleaning up the kitchen that her day changed.

Warren stood next to her before she had a chance to leave and said, "Before you go, I need your help. Amelia's latest dessert is incredible but there's something missing."

Rina froze as she stared at the small ginger cake she'd made that he'd placed in front of her. She'd made it a few days ago and was surprised he hadn't eaten it yet. "I don't think—"

He held out a fork. "Just a small taste. Tell me what you think." He winked. "You'll help me look clever."

She didn't usually like to eat with anyone, but this

didn't count. He only wanted her opinion. Rina sighed and picked up the fork and took a bite.

He watched her. "Well?"

She inwardly sighed recognizing her failing. "Too much ginger."

He snapped his fingers then pointed at her. "I thought so too at first, but I don't think so. It gives a nice bite that's balanced by the hint of ginger wine. It's something else."

She couldn't believe he'd disagreed with her. But his analysis seemed sound. His suggestions had been spot on before. She sat down and took another bite and thoughtfully chewed. She met his gaze. "Stop that."

"What?"

"Watching me."

"I want to know what you think. Body language says just as much as words."

The thought of him watching her body at all, even briefly, made her face burn. It reminded her of how she'd first watched him. How she'd studied every motion from the sweep of his tongue over his lips to his fingers wrapped around the croissant. She set the fork down and began to stand. "I think it's too much ginger."

"Coward."

She looked at him and blinked. "Excuse me?"

He lifted an eyebrow, unfazed by her sharp tone. "You heard me. You're going for the easiest explanation. I thought you had more gumption."

She narrowed her eyes. "I have better things to do."

He shrugged unconvinced. "Sure."

She stared at him for a long moment—meeting his

steady gaze. He'd offered her a challenge and wondered if she'd take it. Her pride was pricked enough not to care that he'd manipulated her. She picked up the fork and took another bite determined to figure out why he thought there was something wrong with the ginger cake. It was through her annoyance, a heightened awareness of him standing close to her that she finally honed in on what it was. The cinnamon was a shade overpowering. It left a subtle aftertaste. She inwardly swore, the man was good.

"You know what it is?" he said.

"Yes." She set the fork down. "But I'm not telling you."

"What?"

She stood and walked passed him. "I'm going home now."

He followed her. "Not until you tell me."

"You can figure it out."

"I've been trying to and it's driving me crazy."

"Good."

He grabbed her wrist. "Please tell me."

She yanked her wrist away. "No."

"I'm sorry I called you a coward."

"No, you're not."

"What do I have to do? Beg?" He jumped in front of her, fell on his knees and pressed his hands together. "Please."

She laughed in spite of herself. He looked both adorable and sexy in that position. "Get up."

His expression didn't change, his voice deepened. "Tell me."

Her laughter died on her lips. Not because of the serious expression in his eyes, the eagerness in his gaze, but the way he looked up at her ignited a dangerous longing within her. He didn't loom over her as he usually did, he seemed attainable. She had a reckless desire to pull him close and whisper what he wanted to hear in his ear. She gasped and took a step back, shocked by her feelings. She shook her head. "I should—"

He scooted closer, closing the distance she'd created. "I'll give you the day off tomorrow."

"No."

"Two days."

Her heart pounded. This was how much he loved her cousin. This was how much he wanted to impress her. "It really means that much to you?"

"Yes."

"Because of Amelia?"

He paused. "Truthfully?"

She nodded.

A mischievous smile touched his lips. "I don't like you knowing something I don't."

She really wished he wouldn't smile at her like that. She wished she didn't imagine kissing his lips, wondering if he'd taste like ginger cake.

"Three days and that's my final offer."

Rina took a deep breath. "I'll tell you but you have to get up first."

His grin turned into a full on smile that turned her insides into mush. "Why? I thought you'd like me begging at your feet. I know Amelia would."

Amelia.

It wasn't the mention of her cousin that suddenly brought tears to her eyes. It was the pain of regret. She didn't regret loving him, she couldn't have stopped herself, it was gaining his trust and deceiving him. That guilt weighed heavy on her.

He treated her as a friend, an equal, and she was keeping secrets.

You have to, the rational side of her said. You were helping your cousin, you didn't know it was him.

But once you did, you shouldn't have accepted his offer to cook for him, her heart said.

But it was too late to back down now. She had a couple more weeks and then she could stop.

She had to stop this.

Warren jumped to his feet, alarmed by the sight of her tears. "Whoa. I'm sorry. What is it?"

She wiped away a tear, ashamed. "I'm really happy for you."

He sighed with feigned annoyance. "No need to cry about it." He rested a hand on her shoulder. "You're the reason I'm here."

She shook her head feeling even more miserable. "No, you did this all on your own. I'm nothing."

His tone turned hard. "Don't say that," he said before he pulled her in his arms. "You're more precious than you think."

She squeezed her eyes shut wanting to struggle and pretend she wanted him to let go, but she didn't. Instead she pressed her cheek against his chest. If only she could disappear like a ghost, melt into his arms and feel this warmth forever. He smelled like home.

"Who hurt you Cirina? Who made you feel this way?"

"Nobody." Her voice remained steady, although the tears continued to fall. If only she could learn to love him less.

"You mean a lot to me. Your life is mine, remember? You can trust me."

"I know." She gently pushed him away, keeping her head down. "Cinnamon."

"What?"

She took a deep breath before she lifted her head and met his eyes. "Too much cinnamon. That's what's wrong with the cake."

Warren folded his arms and held her gaze. When he spoke his voice was tender. "I'm not sure there's anything wrong with it anymore."

She wiped her eyes. "I'm sorry. I really should go."

"Is there anything that happened today that you're not telling me? Did Steve—"

"No, it was innocent. Really," she said before she raced out of the room afraid he'd come up with another reason for her to stay.

CHAPTER TWENTY-EIGHT

*W*arren leaned back on the picnic blanket with a satisfied sigh, the memory of the mango cheesecake Amelia had prepared for him still lingering on his tongue.

He and Amelia had decided to enjoy the remaining days of summer at a local park where people were paddling around the lake in the distance, and he heard the laughter of children as they raced across the grass, startling a gaggle of geese and sending them into flight.

Everything about the day felt perfect, from the weather to the food, to the beautiful woman by his side.

What bothered him was that he couldn't rid his mind of the sight of tears filling sad brown eyes. It had been a week since then and Cirina seemed fine, but he couldn't stop thinking about her.

"I'm a very lucky man," he said more for his sake than hers. "My girlfriend's desserts keep my mouth happy for hours."

Amelia gave him a tight lipped smile. "You don't have to keep mentioning it."

He reached across the blanket took her hand in his. "I don't ever want you to think I take you for granted. I don't. Every bite makes me think of you—sweet, moist and delicious."

She squeezed his hand, but her tight lipped smile remained in place.

That was starting to puzzle him. The more he complimented her the less she seemed happy about it. That surprised him. She seemed the type who would like compliments but she'd become moodier lately.

He was saying or doing something wrong and he didn't know what it was. He couldn't figure it out. He wanted to make her happy. He seemed to be failing at that. He hadn't managed to make his ex-wife happy either. And something he'd said had made Cirina cry, which tore at him because he wanted to see her smile more than anything...

Amelia bit her lip. "Isn't there something else about me that you like?"

Warren pushed down a pinch of annoyance. That was a strange question. Did she really need to ask? "Of course. Plenty."

"Like what?"

"You're beautiful and talented plus you bake like a—"

Her tone turned hard. "I said *besides* baking."

He winced. "It's not something you should be ashamed of," he said confused by her tone. Was she insecure about it? "I'm proud of you. I hope you're proud of your skill too. It's quite an accomplishment. Trust me.

You even run a successful business based on your incredible talent. I don't think you should underestimate how big an accomplishment that is. You're so many things. Too many things for a man to describe. I am thankful that I have you in my life. What more could a man want?"

Her smile softened a little and he felt the tension in him ease. Whatever had made her unhappy, he'd managed to smooth over. If only he knew what it had been so that he wouldn't do it again. That's all he wanted. A relationship without drama, a woman he could please, a restful life.

But if he wasn't careful he could ruin things because as much as he wanted to see Amelia happy, he wondered about Cirina more. He knew she and Amelia had grown up like sisters, but anytime he tried to ask more questions about their past Amelia got irritated.

Amelia's family seemed very loving, yet there was something so sad about Cirina. Wounded.

He knew the feeling. He'd worked hard to hide his, but he knew that at any moment the wounds could crack open and bleed.

He probably shouldn't have hugged her. He felt her stiffen in his embrace, and he was surprised by how thin she felt. Fragile. He wanted her to trust him. How could such a talented woman think she didn't matter?

"What about her?"

He turned to Amelia. "Huh?"

"You said 'Poor Cirina.'"

"I did?"

"Yes," Amelia said, daring him to deny it.

"Oh."

"Why were you thinking about her?"

"I've been working her a little hard lately," he lied.

"She's used to it. She looks a little pitiful, but it's fine. Don't worry about it."

Could he tell her that he was worried about Cirina most of the time? Was it only worry or something else? Something more?

Because as much as he loved Amelia's desserts, he was starting to look forward to Cirina's dinners even more.

Steve was right, he'd been jealous. He didn't like the thought of Cirina cooking for anyone else.

"She's not as strong as you think."

Amelia rolled her eyes. "There you go again. Do you know how annoying it is how much you stand up for her?"

"I don't—"

"I told you how hard it's been without Rina at the Private Pastry Chef and you said that she probably needed a break. Three times you mentioned the Jamaican bammy she made you."

"I did?"

"Yes, and you told me how she listened to a song you were working on for a character and gave you feedback."

"Because she did. I've tried to show you—"

"Darling, I respect what you do but I have no interest in childish games."

He sent her a dark look, annoyed by her tone. "I don't just work on games for children."

"Whatever."

"No," he said determined to make her understand.

"The video game industry is enormous. It can rival movies in the scope and genres involved. What I do—"

She waved a dismissive hand. "I know you and your company make background music."

He took a deep breath. He wouldn't get angry at her. Not everyone understood or appreciated what he did.

But Cirina did. He'd caught her listening to the original soundtrack for Final Fantasy VII while she was cooking lunch.

"You're a fan?"

She quickly turned the music off, looking embarrassed. "No."

He turned it back on. "Don't stop on my account."

"I-I just wanted to understand what you did. I looked up the top ten video game composers." She frowned. "How come you're not listed there?"

He grinned at her teasing. "I'm working on it."

"I know you'll make it one day."

Warren shrugged. "I don't care." He'd spent all his childhood trying to be the best, his parents wanted him to be a legend, leave a legacy. He looked at top ten lists and always realized there were people who he admired who were missing; he found little interest in them anymore. Right now all he cared about was creating something amazing and enjoying the moment.

"Anyway I found Nobuo Uematsu and thought I'd listen to some of his work."

Warren rested a hand on his chest. "My inspiration." He motioned to her tablet. "This is only a taste. When you marry it with the architecture of the game you get a full picture of the power of his work."

"Can you show me a game?"

He paused. "That's a dangerous thing to say to me unless you mean it."

"I do."

And to his shock she did. After dinner, when no one could disturb them, he took her to his studio, which was located in the basement and housed his production company. She didn't try to pretend she understood everything he showed her, but he saw the appreciation in her eyes.

She took in the posters on the walls, the workstations and computer screens, and sophisticated microphones. When he put her in front of a game (he decided to show her an adventure game that put more emphasis on the story rather than the game play), she saw the artistry. He could talk freely with her about his ideas and vision for one of the projects he was working on. He'd been so charged after his time with Cirina that he'd tried to share it with Amelia by telling her what he was working on, but she'd yawned in boredom and changed the subject.

But Cirina never got bored. Cirina listened to him talk about his passion to encourage young people from divergent groups to not only be consumers of video games but also creators. He told her how much money they could make without reaching a mainstream audience or having to knock on the doors of large entertainment companies. That smart nimble companies like his and others could make it.

She not only listened as he talked, but she smiled. She smiled in a way that lit her brown eyes and chased the shadows away. Seeing her smile was such a rarity that sometimes Warren found himself talking and not making sense just to keep her smile in place. He didn't care if she thought he was silly. He preferred it.

But not only did she listen, she cared. She'd once surprised him by creating a snack spread of baked pears with walnut and honey and strawberries drizzled with coconut butter for his team that she'd set out in the garden. They were overjoyed by the treat.

She didn't stay and dismissed their praise.

He wasn't sure if it was shyness or something else that made her fade into the background. But although she was quiet Cirina made an impact.

No, Cirina wasn't pitiful.

Cirina was amazing.

Cirina was surprising.

Cirina was...

As he searched for a word her name—Cirina, Cirina, Cirina—swirled in his mind and for a moment Warren felt like he was being sucked into a vortex—a vortex he could no longer fight. Amelia was right. She had every right to be annoyed with him. He talked about Cirina too much and thought about her too much too. And now he knew the reason.

The thought both terrified and freed him.

He sighed in regret. Amelia deserved better. "You're right. I'm not being fair to you. I—"

"It's okay," Amelia suddenly said in a bright voice. "I know you're a kind man and Rina can be so pathetic sometimes."

"No, that's not—"

She quickly started to gather their things. "Let's go

for a walk," she said and Warren watched her as she avoided his gaze. She didn't want to hear what he had to say and part of him didn't want to say it. He didn't want to lose what he had. There was no stain of his past with Amelia.

And there was no chance Cirina could see him as anything more than the broken man she'd met all those years ago.

IT WASN'T FAIR!

Amelia sat in her apartment and angrily made her way through a pint of cookies 'n cream ice cream. Warren had dropped her home a half hour ago, but she was hungry because she'd barely been able to touch any of the items he'd brought with him for the picnic because *she'd* made them. Rina.

And the mango cheesecake, Amelia had pretended to bring with her, made the lunch even worse. She was tired of him fawning over the food. What was so great about it anyway? He had her now, right? Wasn't she enough? And she could cook. Her parents had loved the peach pie she'd made in high school. She could make him a pie. That wouldn't be too hard.

She'd lost her confidence because her cooking teachers had been too particular. They didn't know what they were talking about. She could cook just as well as Rina. She could follow recipes. She didn't burn food anymore and only twice had left eggshells in a mixture. Everyone made mistakes, right?

She didn't need to depend on Rina anymore. Besides, her cousin was getting a little cocky anyway, just like she had with the business. But the business was running just fine without her, although her accountant had hinted that business could be a bit more brisk, but she'd worry about that later. Warren had given her some money to help out. They also had loyal customers. That was all that mattered.

Rina may know about cooking and business, but when it came to men and relationships her cousin knew nothing. This was her domain. Warren was hers.

It was time to get real. Having Rina make each meal made Amelia feel like a third wheel, as if Rina were in the room with them. The way Warren would slowly taste each bite was sexy, but she was too aware that she wasn't the one making him softly moan like that. She didn't like him asking her questions that she couldn't answer such as what cream she used or spice. Like it mattered? Why did it have to matter? But she could fix this.

She'd do better than a pie.

Amelia put the top on the carton of ice cream and stood. A cake would be even better. She would make Warren something scrumptious and then he'd be completely hers.

CHAPTER TWENTY-NINE

Terror.

That was the first emotion that swept through Rina when she saw the white layered cake sitting on Warren's kitchen counter.

It wasn't one of hers.

She hadn't baked it. On the outside it looked fine, but it smelled wrong, too sweet, too much... Rina took a deep breath. Perhaps she was overreacting. Maybe Amelia had improved. She grabbed a knife just to press it against the top icing. It felt as hard as a rock. She tried to cut into the cake and could barely break the surface. She swore, it was worse than she thought.

"What do you think?" Amelia said, sashaying into the kitchen with a proud grin on her face. "Amazing, right?"

"What have you done?" Rina demanded in a harsh whisper.

Amelia shot her a superior smile. "You're not the only

one who can cook. You should have seen Warren's face when I showed up."

"You should have told me—"

"I know what I'm doing. I don't need your help anymore."

"This cake is as hard as—"

"Isn't this great?" Warren said coming into the kitchen with a smile. "Amelia wanted to drop by and surprise me."

"It certainly is a surprise," Rina said in a strangled voice. Maybe she was overthinking it. Maybe the hard surface would give away to a soft interior. She could say it was something Amelia was experimenting with, not every experiment needed to work.

She took a deep breath. It would be okay.

"You two sit down and let me cut this for you," she said, grabbing a cake knife from the drawer.

Warren started to protest, but Amelia said, "That's a great idea," before she looped her arm through his and dragged him to the kitchen table.

Rina made a silent prayer before she cut the cake. But her hopes faded as she sawed her way through. The cake sounded as tasty as cardboard and felt just as dry.

"What's taking so long?" Amelia said.

"We know you're trying to sneak some for yourself," Warren said with a laugh.

Rina could only groan as she placed slices of the cake on plates for them.

As she set the plates on the table, she briefly had the urge to pretend to trip and drop them on the floor. Unfortunately, she'd also have to find a way to ruin the cake on the counter. She took a step back as if she'd just put down a grenade in front of Warren and watched in slow horror as he used his fork to cut through the cake and lifted the piece to his mouth.

He took a bite then paused. He pushed the piece to the corner of his mouth before he said, "Are you sure you made this?"

Amelia beamed. "Yes, of course. Why do you ask?"

"It just..." He swallowed with some effort then grabbed the glass of water Rina held out to him. "It's different."

She frowned. "Different?" She shot Rina a look.

"Awful." He shrugged. "You always wanted me to be honest with you so I will be. It's hard where it should be soft. I don't even know how you managed that, the flavor's too sweet and..." He shook his head. "There's no point in saying anything else." He pushed the plate away. "This experiment was a disaster."

Rina saw Amelia's face change from hurt to outrage and knew things wouldn't end well if she didn't do something.

Rina rushed forward. "It's my fault."

Warren looked at her confused. "Your fault?"

"Yes, I...I asked Amelia to help me with my baking skills and she was working on this surprise for you, I asked her to let me do it instead. I didn't think it would be this bad."

Warren laughed. "That explains it. Stick to cooking, you've got a ways to go with this fine art."

Amelia pushed back her chair and said in a teary voice, "Excuse me," before she ran out of the room.

Rina held up her hand to stop Warren from following her. "Let me talk to her first. I have to apologize."

Moments later she stood outside the powder room and heard Amelia sniffing inside. "Let me in."

"No."

"Open the door. I can't talk to you like this. What if he hears me?" Rina waited a few seconds hoping she could get her cousin to see reason and finally heard the lock turn. Rina stepped inside and saw Amelia's reddened eyes, a handful of tissues gripped in her fist. "I'm sorry."

"I've never been so humiliated in my life," she said. "You have no idea how hard I worked on that cake. How dare he say those things."

"Have you tasted it yet?"

"No, I didn't get a chance before he said those horrible things. I mean it looks beautiful, right?"

"Why did you want to do this?"

"Because I'm sick and tired of hearing him gush over your food. He's *my* boyfriend not yours."

"He's still your boyfriend and actually this gives you a good reason to stop this pretense. You could say you were so hurt by what happened today that you don't feel like baking anymore."

Amelia sniffed, thoughtful. "That's true."

"That way you don't need me anymore."

She dabbed her eyes dry, a tiny smile on her lips. "Yes, that's true too. I like that idea."

"Feel better now?"

"Yes." Amelia turned to the mirror and gasped. "But I can't go back like this. Give me a few minutes, okay?"

Rina nodded and left relieved she'd managed to help her cousin save face.

She returned to the kitchen where Warren jumped up when he saw her. "Is she okay?"

"She's fine. She just hates failing at anything."

Warren frowned. "But she didn't fail, you did."

Rina paused. That's right. She was the one who was supposed to have baked the cake. "Yes, but...initially you thought she had baked it and she had tried to teach me and had failed." She held up both hands. "But everything is fine now. She just needs a few minutes."

Warren rested a hand on his chest. "That's a relief." He folded his arms. "But I want you to tell me the truth."

Rina picked up the plates and froze. "About what?"

"The cake."

She swallowed. "What about it?"

"You got a store display and tried to pass it off as something you created from scratch, right?"

She recognized his teasing and couldn't stop a smile. "Shut up." She walked past him and dumped the cake slices in the trash.

He leaned against the counter and his eyes continued to dance with amusement. "I thought you were good at anything in the kitchen, but you were terrible at this."

She lifted a knife and waved it at him. "I said shut up."

He sniffed. "You think that's scary? Threaten to pick up that cake and throw it at me. That'd have me running."

"Do you want any dinner tonight?"

He lifted a brow. "You're threatening not to cook for

me now? I'd actually pay you never to bake something again."

Rina folded her arms. "You're enjoying this, aren't you?"

He grinned. "Very much. You were a little too close to perfect."

"I'm far from perfect."

He motioned to the cake. "And this is proof."

Rina grabbed a chunk of the cake. "I should shove this in your mouth."

"You'd have to catch me first."

She threw the cake at him. It hit him square in the chest.

He glanced down at the big, sticky stain before he gripped the front of his shirt and stumbled forward. "Death by cake. I never thought this would be my end. Tell Amelia..." He collapsed forward then lay still.

Rina laughed.

A few yards away, Amelia stood, watching them and seethed with anger. They were laughing. They were both laughing at her!

How could they do this to her?

She watched Warren jump up and clean off the front of his shirt. He was never that playful with her. She sensed that something was going on between them.

She wasn't going to be made a fool of again. She was smarter than people gave her credit for. She wouldn't be tossed aside. Especially not for Rina. Rina who pretended to care, but then made fun of her behind her back. Rina who probably wanted Warren for herself.

But she wouldn't let her have him.

She walked into the kitchen. "You're having fun without me?"

"Just admiring your cousin's culinary skills," Warren teased. He unbuttoned his shirt and looked down. "I think she left a bruise."

Rina nudged him, awkward. "That's enough."

Amelia forced a laugh. "It's amazing she cooks anything at all considering she hardly eats anything."

Warren frowned. "What?"

She rested against the kitchen island and sent Rina a look. "Does he know about you and a little thing called 'rehab'?"

Rina didn't move, not understanding the vicious look in her cousin's eyes. Why was she bringing that up? It wasn't something she wanted anyone to know, especially Warren.

"Everything is fine now," Rina said in a low voice. "There's nothing to worry about."

But Amelia didn't seem to care. She shifted her gaze to Warren and said, "Yeah, she spent months there. Before that she briefly had a feeding tube. Maybe that's how she lost her sense of taste."

Warren's eyes turned hard. "That's enough."

"I'm only getting started. She's not as amazing as you think. She's struggled with an eating disorder for years."

Icy contempt flashed in his eyes. "So what?"

Amelia blinked shocked by the fierceness of his gaze. He'd never looked at her like that before. It frightened her.

She licked her lips, her mouth dry. "I just—"

He took a step towards her. "I know."

"You do?"

"Yes, she—"

Rina looked at him in a panic. She'd never told him about rehab and Amelia couldn't know that they'd met in the hospital. "No, please don't—"

Amelia's eyes darted between the two of them, catching the quick look they shared. "What are you two hiding from me?"

"Nothing," Rina said.

"Did she already tell you? Have you been sharing secrets?"

"No, it's nothing like that," Rina tried to assure her.

"That's right," Warren said. "I didn't know Cirina's past. I didn't know she was in a rehabilitation facility, but if you think that would matter to me you're wrong. It makes me admire her even more."

Amelia stared at him. It wasn't what he'd said that enraged her, it was what he didn't say. It was that protective look in his eyes. He was protecting Rina. He was showing his feeling for her.

She would make him pay.

She'd hurt him before he could hurt her.

CHAPTER THIRTY

The last thing Steve remembered before he woke up next to a half naked Amelia was that his drink tasted funny.

He'd come over to her apartment after she'd called him and told him she needed his help setting up a surprise for Warren.

This was not the kind of surprise Steve had in mind.

He rubbed his eyes and shook his head to make sure he wasn't dreaming.

He didn't have a headache, but his mouth felt dry. That still wasn't proof of anything. He pinched himself.

No, he wasn't dreaming. He looked around at the pink floral prints on the wall and then the foot of the iron sleigh bed before he glanced at the woman soundly asleep beside him. He was clearly in a nightmare.

There was no way he could have slept with his best friend's girl. Absolutely no way. He'd done some dumb things in his life, but he had a code.

Besides, if he'd wanted to poach anything Warren had it would have been Rina, not Amelia.

He shuddered at the thought. The woman was gorgeous; there was no questioning that as he let his gaze sweep over her luscious figure, her breasts and bottom covered in the flimsiest of black lace.

But there was no way he'd crossed that line.

Okay, so it was true that his memory was fuzzy (he really couldn't remember anything) and sure his trousers were hanging on the doorknob (right above his shirt that was crumbled on the ground) but that didn't mean anything.

Steve took a deep breath before he slid out of the bed as slowly as he could. Since he'd done so before (more times than he could count) he'd become almost a master at it (he was certain he could place a full glass of wine next to himself and get out of bed without spilling a drop).

Amelia shifted and mumbled something, but didn't arouse from her sleep. Success.

He stood and carefully gathered his clothes before he left the room, closing the door behind him.

That was too close. He quickly pulled on his jeans before putting on his shirt; he'd button it up once he found his shoes. He searched her apartment wondering where they could be, he had a sinking feeling that he might have left them in her bedroom (too bad he wasn't going back) before he noticed them halfway under the couch. How they'd gotten there was anyone's guess.

He put them on, grabbed his jacket, making sure his

keys were still inside the pocket (they were, yes!), before he opened the front door and stifled a scream.

Warren stood there.

With Rina.

Warren held his hand as if he were about to knock. He slowly let his hand fall as he let his gaze sweep over Steve's unbuttoned shirt and untied shoes. Warren lifted an eyebrow. "Should I even ask?"

"What are you doing here?"

"You first."

"Look, she's still asleep. I'll explain on—"

"Steve is that you?" Amelia said, coming into the room wrapped in a silk robe.

Steve closed his eyes and swore.

"Now it gets interesting," Warren said.

"I thought I heard voices," Amelia said then stopped when she saw Warren. She covered her mouth in shock. "Oh, you're here."

Rina stuck her head out from behind him. "Cut it out, Amelia."

Her look of surprise turned to anger. "You're not supposed to be here."

"Let's not have this conversation in the hallway."

"This is none of your business." She glared at Warren. "What are you doing with her?"

He stepped inside and nodded to Steve. "Not what you've been doing with him."

Steve waved his hands. "Nothing happened."

"Why are you doing this?" Rina asked her.

Amelia's eyes flashed. "Go home, Rina, this has nothing to do with you."

"But everything to do with me, right?" Warren said. "That's why you called me?"

Steve turned to her. "You called him?"

"I thought he should know about us."

Steve shook his fists. "There is no *us*!"

Amelia walked up and touched Steve's chest. "But you were amazing last night."

He jerked back as if she'd burned him. "I didn't do anything!" He turned to Warren and Rina, his eyes pleading. "I would remember."

"We believe you," Rina said.

Warren looked at her. "We do?"

"Yes." She folded her arms. "I don't know why she wants to make you jealous." She looked at her cousin. "But Amelia, choosing to seduce a gay man isn't the wisest choice."

"Gay?" Warren and Steve said in unison.

"You would have done better with another strategy," Rina continued.

"I'm not gay," Steve said.

Rina frowned. "Are you sure?"

Warren started to laugh.

He shot his friend a look. "Of course I'm sure."

"So you're not the former groundskeeper who's in love with Warren?"

"You have a groundskeeper in love with you?" Amelia said.

Warren shook his head. "He made a pass."

"I told you I was a game designer," Steve said.

Rina scratched her cheek. "I know you did, but I thought maybe you were lying."

He turned to Warren. "You didn't tell her about me?"

Warren sniffed. "Why would I do that?"

"Because we're friends." He looked at Rina. "I wouldn't lie. Why would I lie?"

Rina rested a hand on her hip. "Because you didn't want Warren to know you were there, remember? I had to stop you from hiding in the shower."

Amelia's eyebrows shot up. "You two were in a shower together?"

"No, we—"

Warren held up his hands. "Stop." He took a deep breath. "Cirina, Steve, I need to talk to Amelia alone."

Steve pressed his hands together. "But I—"

"Now." Warren pulled out his car keys and handed them to Rina. "I'll be there shortly."

Amelia pointed at the keys, outraged. "You came here together! In the same car?!"

"Go," Warren said in a soft voice.

Rina sighed before she followed Steve out the door.

"I can't believe you brought her with you. It's like you can't live without her."

"I brought her with me, along with a breakfast spread she'd made for us. We were going to surprise you. She'd wanted to make up for the cake fiasco, although I'd told her it wasn't necessary."

He took a seat. "She was trying to save our relationship, not realizing there was nothing to save."

Amelia's eyes filled with tears.

"I didn't realize it until this moment. I was still willing to try. I felt guilty." He flashed a cold smile. "But you freed me."

"You heartless bastard."

His cold smile spread wider. "Do you really want me to start calling you names?"

"Get out," she said in a broken whisper.

"Because I won't. Do you want to know why?"

She raised her voice. "I said get out."

He didn't move. "I feel sorry for you. You have so much and don't even see it. You kept calling your cousin pathetic, never realizing you were talking about yourself."

She slapped him.

Hard enough to make her palm burn. She'd never slapped a man, before not even her ex when she'd found out he'd been cheating on her. But he hadn't made her feel like this. To feel this anger. Pathetic? He dared call her pathetic? She was Amelia Parker. She had money, had gone to the best schools, owned a successful business and looks that turned men's heads and yet this man...

This horrible man she'd allowed herself to love had tossed her aside for her scrawny, plain cousin?

Slapping him wasn't enough. She wanted to punch him with all her might. Leave him with bruises and wipe the disdain from his eyes.

"You're the pathetic one," she said. "I know about the scars." She sniffed in delight when she saw a touch of fear enter his gaze. "I may not know how you got them, but I know they run deep. I know you sometimes have night-mares; you whisper a woman's name in your sleep. I know you pretend to be strong, but that you're weak. You can't handle a woman like me. You think I haven't notice you wince when I move too fast or catch you off guard? What do you think Rina will say?"

He slowly rose to his feet. "I don't care as long as I no longer have to pretend that I love you."

Amelia lifted her hand again, but this time he stopped her, capturing her wrist in an iron grip. "I allowed the first one," he said in a velvet whisper. "The second one will cost you."

She yanked her hand free. "It won't work. You can't be with Rina. You think you're so smart but she's been deceiving you all this time."

"Deceiving me?"

"Yes. She's been lying to you for months right under your nose. I didn't make those desserts for you, she did."

He hesitated. "I know."

Amelia blinked. "You know? You knew it all along?"

"You may think I'm weak, but you should never assume I'm stupid." He turned and walked out the door, leaving Amelia speechless.

CHAPTER THIRTY-ONE

He'd been bluffing.

Warren stumbled out of Amelia's apartment in a state of shock. He hadn't known. Not for certain at least. He'd sensed something was off, but he'd never suspected this.

Rina had been lying to him all this time?

He slowly walked down the corridor in a daze as Amelia's revelation settled in his mind. Rina had made the desserts. He'd trusted her and all this time she'd been deceiving him with food. He'd brought her into his home, into his confidence, trusted her as a friend and she'd used him. Used him for a job, used him to help her cousin make him fall in love with her.

He'd fooled himself into thinking that she really cared for him. But how could she, knowing his past? Amelia didn't know the details and thought he was pathetic.

Cirina did. Cirina knew the truth in all its ugliness.

He briefly closed his eyes, wishing he'd let Amelia hit him again. It would have felt good. Almost right. That kind of pain he understood. For years it was the kind of pain he'd grown used to. Not this.

Not the pain of letting someone in close and realizing they didn't care at all.

He didn't know how long it took him to reach his car, but each step took effort.

Rina jumped out of the car when she saw him. "I saw Steve leave. Are you okay?"

"I'm fine," was all he was able to manage. He drove home in silence and Rina was wise enough to not ask him any questions. She sent him nervous glances, but that was all.

Once they reached his house, he helped her put the breakfast spread in the refrigerator.

"You can't leave me in suspense," Rina said, closing the refrigerator door. "Tell me what happened."

Warren rested his palms on the cool counter top, hoping it could somehow ease the burning anger inside him. He kept his gaze on his hands, unable to look at her. "When were you going to tell me?" he said in a quiet voice.

"Tell you what?"

"Amelia told me about the desserts."

He heard her gasp and waited for a series of denials. But they didn't come. Silence surrounded them.

"Did you have fun? Must have been hilarious."

Rina shook her head, her voice filled with misery. "She shouldn't have...why would she..." She swallowed. "She cares about you."

He closed his eyes. "So the answer is never. You were never going to tell me."

"No."

He nodded. "I see."

"You were never supposed to find out." He heard her take a step towards him then stop, sensed her reaching out to him before pulling away. He squeezed his eyes even tighter. He didn't want to imagine the pity in her gaze, feel the worry in her touch.

"I didn't know it was you."

"What?"

"When she first asked me to help her I didn't know it was you and then when I found out it was too late."

Warren pushed himself from the counter and spun to face her. "Too late for what? You lied to me for months! Not days, not weeks. Months! You pretended to care—"

"I did care. I *do* care. I wanted to see you happy. It was a minor deception."

His voice cracked. "Minor?"

"I'm not saying what I did was right, I'm sorry, but don't tell me it was the only reason you fell in love with Amelia. You fell in love with her because she's beautiful, successful, clever, and she has a generous heart."

Warren folded his arms, his eyes darkened. "A generous heart? You really think that?"

"I know it. Amelia can appear shallow at first, but there's more to her than you think. She was kind to me as a child, she was the brains behind the Private Pastry Chef, she was the one who fell for you so completely she wanted to treat you to a special dessert every month. That was her idea not mine, she just didn't have the skill to do it so she asked for my help. And I wanted to help her. In the meantime she was taking lessons to improve and—"

"Do you think Amelia loves me?"

Rina took a hesitant step towards him, her eyes pleading for him to understand. "Yes, she loves you very much. I don't know what she said to you today, but it was out of hurt and anger, but it doesn't reflect how she really feels. Give her some time and whatever misunderstanding you had can—"

"There's no misunderstanding," Warren said. "I'm never seeing her again and she feels the same."

"Let me talk to her. You two were so happy together."

His mouth pulled into a sour grin. "You don't know your cousin as well as you think."

"I do. She—"

He took a step towards her. "If she truly has such a generous heart why did she mention your time in rehab?"

Rina took a wary step back. "I told you she was upset."

Warren took another step forward. "Why did she try to set up my best friend?"

Rina took two steps back and forced a laugh. "She can be overly dramatic."

"Why did she have to mention that you made the desserts? I wouldn't have known that."

"I don't know!"

"I do." Warren grabbed her shoulders and his dark gaze pinned her in place, allowing no resistance. "Because she wanted to hurt me. Because she knows how I feel about you and Steve. How precious you both are to me. She said and did those things because she's not as caring and thoughtful as you want to believe." He bit his lip. "I know this Cirina because I made those same excuses before with Myra."

Rina pulled away from him, disgusted. "No, Amelia is nothing like that."

"It certainly felt the same when she hit me."

Rina stared at him openmouthed.

He nodded at her horror and disbelief.

She covered her mouth with a trembling hand, and whispered, "No," with a note of anguish he'd never heard before.

Warren swore. "Cirina, it's okay. I shouldn't have said anything. It wasn't that big of a deal. I provoked her and—"

Her eyes filled with tears. "You were never supposed to be hurt again. You two were so perfect together. This is my fault."

"Cirina stop it. This is not your fault."

"Aunt Sonia said I was poison. I ruined—"

"You didn't ruin anything."

"She would have never done that if it weren't for me. She was so hurt after the cake. I haven't seen her that miserable in a long time. I can fix it."

"Cirina, I don't want you to fix anything. I'm not broken. You treat me as if I'm a toy that needs mending. You did the same all those years ago. You think you know what's best for everyone around you."

She shook her head. "That's not true."

"You made me look like a fool. If you cared for me even a little—"

"Cared? You think I don't care? You have no idea how much it hurts me to love you!"

He gaped at her. "What?"

She gripped her shirt, tears stinging her eyes. "I endured months of pleasure and agony for you. I wanted to get over you. But I couldn't. Even when I knew I didn't have a chance with you. You said so yourself when you hired me. There was no chance of you seeing me any other way. But from the moment that orange rolled into my hospital room, I saw you as someone amazing. I never meant to hurt you. I made a promise I'd never let you know, especially when I knew you loved someone else. That you'd never be attracted to me, you said so yourself."

"I was wrong," Warren said in a fierce whisper before he cupped her face in his hands and covered her mouth with his own.

CHAPTER THIRTY-TWO

Could this be happening? Was this a dream?

Rina didn't dare move under the sensual assault. She kept her arms by her side, her feet planted, afraid that if she moved she would awaken.

But as the kiss deepened, the taste of his lips an intoxicating flavor she couldn't place, she felt her arms rise and circle him. He felt real, solid, warm. The warmth she'd always imagined being wrapped around her was suddenly real and even better. It came with so many other sensations—the scent of honey, the soft cotton of his sweater, the sound of his beating heart. The touch of his lips, so warm and wet.

He hadn't pushed her away. She wasn't invisible.

"Stay with me," he said.

It was too soon, she told herself. He was getting over Amelia. He was vulnerable right now, she shouldn't take advantage.

But her traitorous body didn't care. It wanted this.

Craved it. Needed it. She didn't hesitate when he led her to his bedroom. She didn't tremble when he closed the door behind him or when he slowly slipped out of his clothes.

She sat on the side of the bed and hungrily watched him just as she had when she'd seen him at the bakery eating. There was no motion that didn't capture her attention, the shape of his body, the color of his skin, the movement of his muscles. He was beautiful. She swallowed him up with her eyes. He stopped before he pulled off his briefs.

He grinned. "Is this supposed to be a strip show?"

She blinked. "I'm sorry?"

He motioned to her clothes. "Planning to stay like that?"

"Yes."

His grin fell. "What? Really?"

"Just for a little longer." She got under the covers and licked her lower lip, hoping he wouldn't find her strange. "Can I...can you get in bed and let me just touch you first?"

He narrowed his eyes, uncertain. "Are you serious?"

"Yes," she said eager, her heart racing. This might be her only chance and she didn't want to miss it.

Warren sent her a look then slid under the covers beside her. "Like this?"

"Yessss," Rina hissed suddenly feeling like a powerful snake sliding its body around its prey. He was hers now. Rina shifted closer to him and sighed with pleasure as his warm body pressed even closer to hers. She wasn't alone.

She wasn't a ghost.

She was alive, vital, powerful. Every touch of her fingers against his flesh felt electric, the scent of his skin sent her senses spinning, but the taste of him was even better. She let her tongue trail a leisurely path down his chest, capture a nipple in her teeth, suck the side of his neck like a vampire. It was heaven. He was as sweet as grater cake, and for a moment she was a child again on a Jamaican beach realizing she wasn't alone in the world.

Her hunger for him knew no bound. If she could devour him she would.

Warren cleared his throat. "Uh Cirina..."

"Hmm?"

"You may not have noticed but in a couple seconds I could shoot off like a rocket."

She frowned. "A rocket?"

His voice deepened. "I'm certainly as hard as one."

She grinned, sweeping her hand over his body in admiration. "You certainly are."

He glanced down. "Especially a certain part of me."

Rina followed his gaze and belatedly noticed his erection. "Oh, sorry." She sat up and backed away from him, embarrassed. "I got carried away." She couldn't believe she'd been so selfish.

"It's okay," Warren said with a chuckle. "But I'd like to join in on the fun."

"Right. You're not having any fun."

"I didn't say that." He grabbed a condom from his side drawer. "It's just I'd like to be a little more involved."

"Okay." She removed her blouse and Warren had to fight not to stare as she unlatched her bra. He knew she was thin, but he didn't expect her to be as small as she was. For a second he was afraid to touch her, as if she might break. Damn, he suddenly felt enormous beside her. His gaze shifted from the protruding bones of her collarbone and hip. Did she eat at all?

"What's wrong?"

"Nothing."

She smiled but it was a little sad. "You don't have to pretend. It must be a shock to go from beautiful Amelia to me."

He tenderly cupped her face. He wouldn't lie to her and tell her she was beautiful, she wasn't and she didn't need to be. She was something so much more, especially to him, with a beauty uniquely her own. He winked. "Mind being on top?"

"Top?"

"I like a woman who likes to take control."

The shadow of sadness left her face and he was rewarded with an expression of joy that filled him with a warm glow.

She'd said she loved him, he never would have guessed. He'd thought she pitied him, saw him as weak, and yet...she touched him with reverence.

He'd heard the words "I love you" said many times before. But for the first time in his life, he believed them. He believed her.

Not because he wanted too, even though he did, but because of the way she looked at him.

Her heart shone bright in her eyes. The same love he'd seen when she was in the kitchen, when he used to watch her when she wasn't looking; when she'd hand him a dish she'd made, pride beaming in her gaze.

One day he'd find out why she deprived herself. One day he'd coax her into eating more, but right now he didn't care if he needed to be a piece of meat in front of a cheetah; prey to her predatory need. He wanted her to feel strong. He wanted her to take charge and know that her power was something he could handle.

"I'll be gentle," she said as she saddled him, fitting him inside her.

He sucked in a breath feeling her tight, wet muscles surround him in liquid heat. "You'd better not be," he said in a voice that didn't sound like his own.

And she wasn't. She was reckless and wild rocking them both into heightened ecstasy. She said his name.

He could barely speak.

She gasped.

He groaned.

Soon he wanted more too, he wanted to feel her squirm beneath him; he wanted to feel her panting breath hot against his neck. His hands roamed over every intimate inch of her flesh.

Rina moaned and shivered in delight. His touch electrified every sense. She'd gotten used to being pushed away, overlooked, discarded. But Warren made her skin tingle, her body vibrate. Not only was she not alone, he wanted her there.

He wanted her.

She belonged in his bed.

She belonged in his arms.

She finally felt she truly belonged somewhere.

PART IV

"And the day came when the risk to remain tight in a bud was more painful than the risk it took to blossom."

Anais Nin

CHAPTER THIRTY-THREE

For the next two days no one could reach them.

They spent most of their time in bed, in the shower, in the bath, or in the garden, sharing a hammock.

Rina had started to drift off to sleep, lulled by the warmth of his body, the gentle early autumn breeze and the multi-hued sky above when she heard Warren softly swear.

She looked at him alarmed. "What?"

"I just realized I have to fire my chef."

She playfully swatted his chest. "You don't have to fire me. We can go on as if nothing's happened."

"You're kidding, right?"

"No, I'm not."

"I can't do that."

"You did it before when we met after seven years. You looked at me as if we'd never met."

"I thought you'd forgiven me for that."

She tapped the side of her head. "Forgiving doesn't mean forgetting."

He groaned. "Do we have to?"

"Yes."

"I don't want to pretend nothing's happened. I don't want to pretend that I don't want you to wrap your legs around me and scream my name."

"Shut up."

"Or strip you naked and cover you in chocolate."

She covered his mouth. "I said shut up."

He moved her hand. "Whipped cream? Strawberries?"

She closed her eyes.

"You can do the same to me."

A soft smile curved her lips. "Don't worry, I plan to."

"The way you go at me in bed, I'm not sure they'll be anything left."

She opened her eyes. "Relax, I know how to make things last." She narrowed her eyes and pointed at him in warning. "But nobody can know about this."

"I didn't plan to record bedroom scenes and post it anywhere."

"That's not what I mean and you know it. We have to be careful. At least for a couple months, no one can know about us. Think about how it will look."

"I don't care."

"I do. Amelia may be your ex-girlfriend but she's still my cousin."

Warren understood her reasoning, but still didn't like

the idea of his girlfriend working for him. However, for the next week he kept his distance whenever anyone was around. They'd almost gotten caught by Steve who had been helping Warren in the studio and had come to the kitchen looking for Warren and had nearly seen Warren steal a kiss before Warren pretended to walk past Rina. Rina made an offhanded statement about having to go shopping before she left.

Steve held up a book featuring a black woman holding a magical dagger. "Where did you get this? I saw it on the porch."

"It's not mine, it's Cirina's."

"But how? It's not in stores yet. This is an Advance Reading Copy."

"So?"

Steve waved the book. "And it's signed," he said amazed. "How did she get it?"

"How much is it worth to you?"

"I'm serious."

"Me too."

"I've been trying to get a hold of this author without any luck. She gives cursory replies to my emails. Her stories are amazing. She has this series about this woman who's a psychologist by day—"

"And a demon fighter by night," Warren guessed.

"Sort of. She's able to fight the dark forces that take over her patients. I'm not summarizing it right, but it's interesting. I want to turn her books into a game. I just need a chance to talk to her."

"I'll let Cirina know and see if she can help."

"Tell her I'd kneel at her feet."

Warren shook his head. "I'm not telling her that. But I will tell her why you're interested."

"Thank you. I'm counting on you."

Warren did ask Rina about the book later that day as they cleaned up the dinner dishes and pots. He'd managed to convince her to sit with him, although she still didn't feel comfortable eating with him yet, and had grown used to him helping her out afterwards. She pulled off her dish washing gloves and laughed at Warren's imitation of Steve's enthusiasm. "I'm not sure my sister will go for it," she said, "but I'll try."

"The author is your sister?"

"Yes." Rina pointed at his delighted expression. "But don't tell him that. I think he'd become impossible and I can't make any promises."

Warren's gaze darkened and he gently brushed his hand against her cheek. "Why are you forcing me to keep so many secrets?"

Rina looked down feeling suddenly flustered. She hadn't gotten used to his touches yet. "Only two."

He frowned. "You don't like when I do that."

She lifted her gaze. "What?"

"Touch you. You stiffen every time I do it."

"No, it's not that." She'd never been with anyone so affectionate before. She liked it but it was also a little unsettling. The one boyfriend she'd had after leaving rehab, a man who'd barely lasted five minutes in bed, rarely kissed her let alone touched her with any interest outside of the bedroom. "I like it...I'm not used to it. I'll try harder."

He pressed a soft kiss on the back of her neck. "You don't have to try anything. Be yourself."

Rina took a deep breath. Yes, she could do that. He was affectionate; he probably wanted her to be affectionate too. She grabbed the front of his shirt and meant to pull him close for a kiss, but instead she surprised him and he jerked back, pulling her forward. She lost her balance and ended up butting him in the mouth with her forehead.

They both stumbled back in pain.

Warren rubbed his mouth. "Forget what I said. Don't be yourself, be someone else."

Rina squinted at him, her head throbbing. "I'm so sorry."

"What the hell was that?"

"I was trying to be spontaneous like you."

"Spontaneous?"

"Yes, you're always finding ways to be romantic and sweet."

Warren wrapped an arm around her waist and drew her close before he touched the tip of his tongue against her lips. "You mean like this?" he said his breath hot against her mouth.

"Show off."

He flashed a superior grin. "Honey, I'm a master. Don't even try. Besides, I like you just the way you are, except when you're using your head as a battering ram."

She bit her lip. "I'm really sorry about that." She reached to touch his face then stopped and gripped her hand into a fist.

His eyes searched her face. "How come you only feel comfortable touching me in bed?"

She felt her face burn. He wouldn't understand if she told him. He was like a toy she didn't want to wear out. She didn't want to overwhelm him, seem too needy. "I don't know."

He squeezed her waist before he released her. "It's okay. Don't look at me like that. I'm not angry." He furrowed his brows. "But you're reaching my limit."

She felt her pulse quicken. "You have a limit?"

"I don't like keeping too many secrets."

Rina released a breath, relieved he wasn't talking about reaching a limit with her.

"I want you to meet my brother Peter. You always keep missing each other when he stops by."

Rina cleared her throat. "Actually, I already met him."

"Really? When?"

"I used to work at Bee Sweet years ago."

He paused, pensive. "That's right. The bakery. You approached my table. That's where we met again. His ex still runs it."

"Ex?"

"Yes, Peter caught him baking bread in someone else's oven, if you get what I'm saying. So he got a divorce."

"Oh good," Rina said but when Warren sent her strange look she realized she wasn't supposed to know about Julian's affair with the bread baker so she quickly said, "I mean...oh goodness how awful."

Warren nodded. "I know. He was pretty broken up

about it but they stayed friendly for the sake of the girls. The company is doing okay, but not great. They used to bake the most amazing muffins and croissants and then the food changed."

"Hmm."

A slow realization came over his face. "Wait...you said you used to work there."

She avoided his gaze. "Uh huh."

"When we met were you still working there?"

"It was my final day. I'd been let go." *Because of your brother.*

"It was you! You were the pastry chef. You're the reason the bakery wasn't the same after you left."

She shrugged. "I wouldn't go that far."

He briefly closed his eyes. "Now it makes sense why the Private Pastry Chef croissant had felt so familiar."

She flashed a small smile. "You forgave me for tricking you, remember?"

He cut her a hurt look. "I'm trying."

"And I won't do it again. But I'd like holding off meeting your brother for a little while longer."

Warren sighed, resigned. "Fine. I'll hold off on anyone knowing about our relationship a little longer," he said, "but I think Steve should know about your sister."

"I don't."

"I do."

"How can I convince you?" Rina tapped her chin, pretending to look pensive. "What if I told you what I plan to make for dessert tonight?"

Warren narrowed his eyes. "It won't make a difference."

"Coconut milk rice pudding. Extra creamy."

Warren folded his arms, but his dark gaze sharpened with interest. "No."

"I might even add rum truffles."

He closed his eyes in surrender. "You win. I won't say a word."

CHAPTER THIRTY-FOUR

She sent her sister a text telling her about Steve's interest in her work, but Elin's reply was less than enthused.

I'm not interested.

You should see his work. It's really good.

I don't know.

At least think about it. I'll send you a link to see what he does.

Fine. What are you up to?

Rina chewed her lower lip. *I'm seeing someone who could get me into trouble.*

He's dangerous?

No, he's Amelia's ex.

Does she know?

Not yet. I don't know how to tell her.

She'll find out eventually, so better now than never.

It may not work out. It's only been a couple months.

Then she doesn't have to know.

Exactly.

But be prepared to tell her if it does.

Rina sighed and put her cell phone away. Her sister was right, if her relationship with Warren deepened as much as she hoped it would, she would have to face the consequences. But for now she liked keeping him a secret.

They kept to the same routine only changing one thing—Rina didn't go home at night.

In his arms she was someone else. In his arms her past melted away. She was not the girl who had been forgotten in the boiler room, the girl her parents had sent away, the one who'd been left behind when her cousin's traveled, the one who'd found herself wandering alone on a beach.

Instead, she was always the happy girl in the kitchen with Mr. CC with sweaty cheeks, aching limbs and a smile on her face.

After their first month together, she allowed herself to trust that Warren's feelings were real, that he wasn't only rebounding from Amelia, that he truly cared for her.

By the second month she felt safe to tell him about her time spent in rehab—the structured schedule, the counselors, the weigh-ins, the food journal she still kept; the friend she'd lost to bulimia, the time she'd been kicked out of the gym.

"But I'm so much better now," she said. She didn't want him to worry about her. Things always turned bad when people started to worry about her. So she didn't tell him about the conflicting thoughts she had about food, that she loved to see other people eat, but she didn't enjoy eating. She didn't tell him about the guilt she used to feel eating at the Parker house knowing her parents and siblings didn't have as much food as they did.

She hadn't spoken to Amelia since the Steve incident and dreaded the moment she had to. One day she'd have to tell her about Warren, but she wanted to stall the inevitable as long as she could.

THAT WEEKEND, THEY SAT WITH A HALF EATEN BOWL of popcorn watching an indie drama on his large flat screen enjoying each other's company and thinking of nothing else when Warren glanced over at Rina and frowned.

"What?" Rina asked.

"Why are you so far away?"

"How can I be far away when I'm sitting right here next to you?"

"You're not right next to me."

She looked at the tiny gap between them. "There's a foot distance between us."

He tipped his head back and shook his body like a toddler with a tantrum. "Why is my girlfriend so far away? I miss her."

Rina poked him in the side. "Warren, stop it."

He shook his body again and lifted his voice in a whine. "Whyyy?"

Rina laughed and closed the distance until their thighs touched. "Better?"

He sat up and rested his arm around her shoulders. "Much."

Rina shook her head as she snuggled against him. He felt so good. "You're such a child."

His gaze traveled over her face. "No," he said in a deep, silken voice that made it clear that he wasn't. "I'm just a man who likes having you close to me."

She lifted her hand to teasingly poke his cheek, but he winced before she touched him.

She drew back; he swore.

"Sorry, about that," he said with regret. "Old habit."

"No, I-I should have warned you."

He swore again, annoyed. "You don't have to warn me, Cirina. You didn't do anything wrong."

He moved his arm from around her shoulder, leaving her feeling cold. When he stretched his arm up, she saw the scar that marred his side, before his sweater hid it again.

He caught her looking and flashed a cynical grin. "You already know how I got that."

She lifted up his sweater and lightly touched his scar with the tip of her finger. "In a way I'm glad."

"You're glad?"

"That night brought you to me." She lowered his sweater and rested her head on his shoulder. "And now you're mine."

CHAPTER THIRTY-FIVE

The Private Pastry Chef is in trouble. I haven't been able to focus since my breakup with Warren. My breakup with Gerry was bad but this was ten times worse. You should have heard the things he said to me. Are you still working for him? You haven't returned any of my calls or responded to my texts. Are you avoiding me? Anyway, the business falling apart is partly your fault, the woman you hired decided to quit. She felt I gave her too much to do. I mean...really? Wasn't that her job? To do what you used to? Anyway, call me when you get this message. I mean it Rina. I need to talk to you.

"What are you going to do?" Warren asked Rina once she'd finished playing the message on her phone.

They sat in his living room, outside his window white clouds blanketed the sky and a cold wind rushed past.

"I don't know."

"You should offer to buy it."

Rina stared at him, shocked by the suggestion. "But it's her company."

"It was her idea, but from everything you've told me, you're the one who made it happen."

Rina chewed her lip. A tinge of excitement coursing through her. She liked the idea of owning the Private Pastry Chef there were things she wanted to do with it that Amelia had never allowed. But she couldn't take it from her. Rina shook her head unsure. "I couldn't do it."

"Why not? I know that you miss it. I don't think you want to be a private chef the rest of your life." He squeezed her hand. "It's okay to say what you want."

It was odd to hear him say that. She'd gotten so used to saying what people wanted to hear from her, she rarely listened to what she truly wanted for herself. She did want the Private Pastry Chef as hers. She wanted to be back in an industrial kitchen among the sights of melted chocolate and whirring sounds of machines. But it felt too much to ask. Too out of reach.

"The branding and everything revolves around Amelia. She has an MBA. I don't."

"You could get around the branding. As far as her degree, you're right. She's smart and knows about business. However, you know more about running the Private Pastry Chef than she does. You should consider buying the company or becoming the president. I know a lawyer who could help you deal with the logistics."

"I still think that's too drastic."

Warren nodded. "Okay, there's another option."

"What?"

"Let it fail."

"I'd hate to see that happen. There are employees who depend on it. Plus, we worked so hard to make it profitable."

"You mean *you* did. You can't keep running in to rescue her. She needs to recognize that. If you don't want to buy her out then tell her you want to run it. She was happier with you running it anyway. If she's honest she wants to move on to something else. Ask her and see what happens."

"Absolutely not!" Amelia said when Rina approached her with the idea at the office. She pointed to her picture on the wall. "This company is mine."

"Think carefully. People's jobs are at risk if—"

"That's why I'm asking for help. Aren't you listening?"

"But I want to be in charge."

"No."

Rina sighed. She hadn't thought it would be easy convincing Amelia and she'd been right. "Okay, if you don't want to sell it what if you let me become president, adjust the partnership structure—"

"No."

"You'd still make money."

"I'm the president. I'm the owner. That won't change." She folded her arms. "How much were you willing to offer anyway?"

Rina picked up a pen and sticky pad. She scrolled down an amount then handed it over to her.

Amelia looked at the amount, her eyebrows briefly raising in shock, before falling again. "Where would you get this kind of money?"

"I have some money saved."

"Not this much."

Rina knew it best not to mention that Warren was willing to help her and also had connected her with a bank willing to offer her assistance. "Plus there are ways. Are you interested?"

Amelia crumpled the note in her fist. "No. When did you get so greedy? First you try to steal my man and now you're trying to steal my business."

"I didn't steal anybody."

"Warren was mine. He loved me, until you seduced him."

"I what?!"

"I don't know how," Amelia said, warming to the idea. "But you did. Are you still working for him? Wait, that's impossible. He probably fired you. He tried to pretend that he knew all along, but I don't believe him. You lost your job, right? Is that why you've been ignoring me?"

Rina bit her lip before she said in a quiet voice, "I still work for him."

"What!"

"And...I'm—"

"So what are you going to do to fix this?"

"Amelia, I'm trying to tell you that—"

"I don't care about your feelings for Warren right now. You can moon over him all you want. It won't work, but if you want to make a fool of yourself that's your business. I wanted you here to help me with mine." She tapped the desk. "This is critical. I don't think we'll last three weeks if we don't do something drastic. What can I do?"

Rina looked around the office before she said in a quiet voice, "Why should I help you?"

"Wh-what?"

"You're right." She swept her hand to encompass to the room. "This is your business. This has nothing to do with me anymore. Why should I help you?"

"Because we're family. That's what families do."

Relatives, Rina could hear Aunt Sonia say. But Amelia's words shook her. Amelia had been there for her. As a child she used to give Rina fun souvenirs from her travels. Through high school she'd give Rina any of the designer clothes she'd gotten tired of. She always tried Rina's different pastry experiments. It had been Amelia's idea of the Private Pastry Chef that had given Rina a renewed purpose after being dismissed from Bee Sweet. In a way the company had saved her.

But she didn't want to spend the rest of her life feeling grateful. That was what Elin had warned her about. That she had a right to her own life. She faced Amelia, trembling inside but knowing what she had to do. "Either you let me buy you out or you let me be president. Those are your choices," she said then left, never suspecting the fury that would follow.

CHAPTER THIRTY-SIX

"God will see that she is punished," Aunt Sonia said, raising her fist to the ceiling. "Such hubris will be dealt with swiftly!"

Amelia continued to cry. She sat in her parents' great room having told them of Rina's betrayal. Her sister, Clara, sat in front of her looking bored, wondering why she'd had to be called to the family meeting. Lauren sat beside her daughter and patted her back, a tad worried that her daughter had gained weight since the last time she'd seen her. Timothy stood by the fireplace, grim faced with his hands in his pockets, while Sonia held court, sitting in the large armchair. "Don't worry," she said. "Something will be done."

Amelia dabbed her eyes with a tissue and sniffed. "After all I've done for her."

Sonia pounded the arm of the chair with her fist. "What we have *all* done. I knew that child had a wicked heart."

"What am I going to do?"

Lauren gently stroked her daughter's hair. "Is it really such a bad idea to let her buy the company, darling? Wouldn't that make things easier for you?"

Amelia stomped her foot and sent her mother a look of outrage. "It's mine. I don't want her to have it."

Lauren bristled at the outburst. "No need to upset yourself, dear."

"I'm already upset, Mom. How can I be any more upset?"

Clara shrugged. "Mom's right. I don't see the big deal. Take the money and find something else to do. You were getting bored with the business anyway. You said you wanted to travel more."

"That's not the point," Aunt Sonia said before Amelia could reply. "Amelia shouldn't be blackmailed into a decision."

Timothy cleared his throat. "I think the term blackmail is a bit excessive."

"She's exploiting Amelia's desperation. There's no other way to see it. Rina's gotten greedy. Overly ambitious. We cannot bend to her will or she will break us."

Clara rolled her eyes and hid a yawn. "There's nothing to break, Auntie. Amelia's business is in trouble. It's not the first time."

"This is different," Amelia said. "I was young all those times before."

Clara sniffed. "You mean you didn't have Rina before."

"At least I tried to build something on my own instead of sliding into a cushy job at Dad's lab."

"I earned my position there."

"Through sperm donation."

Lauren gasped, shaken by her daughter's indelicate words. "Amelia please."

Clara grinned. "I'm surprised you know how sperm works considering you failed biology."

Lauren turned to her other daughter. "Clara that is not appropriate."

"I didn't fail," Amelia said. "I decided to change majors."

"No surprise there. You're always changing your mind about something."

"That's not—"

Sonia surged to her feet and pointed at the two women. "This is exactly what I mean. Rina's influence. She's caused dissension between sisters. She's allowed anger and sorrow to stain our walls. Think of all we have had to endure because of her. The hospital fees, the inpatient care, her family. This latest action has shown us how far her jealousy has taken her. She will ruin us." Sonia pinned Timothy with a hard look. "What are you going to do?"

Timothy took his hands out of his pockets and stared at his sister-in-law confused. "What am I supposed to do?"

"Remind her that she's part of this family. It's her duty to help."

"She's a grown woman. We can't force her."

"Dad," Amelia said in a pitiful voice. "She not only left the company when I needed her most she also tried to steal my boyfriend. Even though he hurt me, she's still working for him."

Sonia shook her head. "I told you dating a musician was no good."

Clara crossed her legs and swung her foot. "Actually, I liked him." When everyone sent her a scolding look she shrugged and looked at her parents. "What? You both thought the same."

Lauren patted Amelia's back when she started to cry again. "Never mind. You'll find someone else."

"Mom's right," Clara said. "Besides, a good looking guy like Warren wouldn't look at Rina anyway, so don't worry about it."

"What am I going to do?" Amelia wailed.

Sonia sat down and folded her arms. "We will force her hand."

Timothy shook his head. "I don't—"

"Are you still helping Isabel and her children?"

"Well, they're hardly children now, but of course we send something to help them make ends meet."

"Perhaps you should stop."

"I think that's going a little far."

"It would be a good wake up call. She's gotten a bit too haughty. She needs to be reminded of where she comes from. If Rina no longer feels part of this family, she should find out what that means."

CHAPTER THIRTY-SEVEN

It was war.

Rina knew by the panicked phone call from her mother that the Parkers had taken swift action to hurt her. Rina hadn't known that the Parkers had been helping her parents and siblings out financially for years.

Now they threatened to stop.

Rina had heard her mother cry only once before when she was very young, but she heard her crying over the phone as she pleaded with her to help them. Rina knew she had to do something. She wasn't exactly sure what yet. She didn't tell Warren. She didn't want him to get involved. If Amelia found out that they were together it would make a bad situation worse. She had to handle this on her own. She told him she needed some time away to think things through about buying the Private Pastry Chef and he believed her.

Giving her the space to face her family drama alone.

As she walked up the stairs to her parents' apartment

(the elevator was broken again) she couldn't help but notice that the sounds were almost the same—the shouting from one door, the scent of something sweet wafting from another, a child crying. It was as if time had stood still.

As Rina walked down the dark hall, she knew this place could have been her entire existence. She never would have had a garden to play in, plenty of food to eat.

She stopped in front of the worn door and heard something metal clatter to the ground. Jenny must be in the kitchen again.

Rina knocked and heard muffled voices before Jenny's husband opened the door. He didn't smile at her. He wasn't a man who smiled often. He turned and sat beside her mother in front of the TV. Her brother sat by her mother's feet, he still barely spoke, but his eyes lit up in recognition when he saw her and she smiled at him, while her two nephews ages four and three, barely lifted their heads to acknowledge her, too focused on the game they played on their mother's cell phone.

"I'm so glad you could come," her mother said.

Rina bent down and kissed her cheek, briefly inhaling the scent of cheap shampoo and baby oil.

"Your father will be sorry he missed you."

Jenny stormed into the room. "What have you done?"

Rina frowned at her sister's fury. "I haven't done anything."

"Then why aren't the Parkers going to help us anymore? Uncle Timothy said you did something really bad."

"It's...complicated."

"Then I'll make it simple for you. They give us money and now they won't because of you."

"How much do you need?"

Jenny's lip curled. "You really are clueless, you know that? If it were that easy do you think Mom would have called you? I told her she shouldn't. You're useless. You come here with your fancy clothes and think that the money you send is enough. You're as bad as Elin. You both think you're better than us."

"That's not true."

"Did you really think you needed to come down here and visit us? Is that supposed to help us somehow?"

"Jenny, stop it," their mother said.

"It's true. You always come and go as you please never really caring how hard it is for us."

"That's not fair," Rina said. "When I got my apprenticeship at that bakery, I said there was a job you could take."

"As a dishwasher! I didn't want to work in some stupid kitchen!"

"At least it was something and you could have trained for something else."

"It was stupid and didn't pay enough."

"I also told you about the filing and data entry job at Uncle's lab."

"Who wants to be stuck in an office all day?"

"Then there was the sales clerk position at the boutique."

Jenny rolled her eyes. "Kissing ass to a bunch of spoiled rich women."

"I even made up a position for you at the Private Pastry Chef three years ago—"

"I told you I don't want to work in a kitchen. And do you think it would have been easy to move when my man's got a job down here and two babies in tow?"

"He could have found something and—"

"Why do you think you know what's best for me? For everyone?" She tapped her chest. "I had dreams too you know, but I was stuck here, having to take care of everything by myself. So I don't need your high and mighty advice. Either give us what we need or get out. We don't need your pity."

She turned and stormed into the kitchen, which was only a few yards away so Rina could see and hear her banging pots and slamming cupboards.

"She's under a lot of stress," her mother said. "Don't take it personally."

Rina couldn't move. For the first time she saw hate in her sister's eyes. She'd never imagined that all the time she'd been helping them; her sister had despised her for it.

Rina looked around the apartment that seemed even smaller than she'd remembered as a child. She could see the silent fury in her sister's stance. The weariness in her mother's eyes. The lost look in her brother's, the innocence of her nephews, and sensed the seething resentment from her brother-in-law.

She couldn't win this battle that the Parkers had started.

She couldn't ignore and walk away from this misery.

She knew this misery too well.

And she knew how to stop it, at least for a little while. If she helped Amelia it would all fade away.

If she did as Amelia wanted everything would settle into its regular order.

Aunt Lauren and Uncle Timothy would respect her again.

Aunt Sonia wouldn't hint she was going to burn in hell.

Jenny wouldn't feel burdened by responsibilities.

Her parents would get the support they needed.

The employees at the Private Pastry Chef wouldn't lose their jobs.

Everyone would be happy again.

Except her. She'd quietly shoulder her own lonely misery as she always had.

"Don't worry, Mom," Rina said loud enough so that her sister could hear her over the TV and the banging pots. "I'll do something."

CHAPTER THIRTY-EIGHT

*W*here are you?

Rina stared at the text from Elin in surprise. She'd been sitting in her car ready to call Amelia when her sister's text came through.

I'm at Mom and Dad's.

Why?

Things are bad, but I can fix it.

Don't do anything yet.

I have to call Amelia.

No. I need to see you.

Rina blinked. Her sister had never said that before. She hadn't seen her since they were children. She felt both frightened and excited at the same time.

Why?

Go straight home. I'll see you at 11 AM tomorrow. Don't talk to anyone, don't text, don't email, don't call. Don't do ANYTHING!!

Rina chewed her lip. It wasn't like Elin to be so adamant. *Can I talk to Warren?*

Only if you trust him.

I do.

Give me his number.

Why?

Just give me his number. I'll explain everything tomorrow.

She knew Elin was mysterious but this was down-right odd. But at least she wanted to see her. Amelia and Jenny hated her right now anyway, it couldn't get much worse than that. She sent her Warren's number, wondering what her sister could possibly want to talk to him about.

Elin's reply gave Rina no clue to her intentions she simply typed *Thanks. Now go home,* before she disconnected.

SHE THOUGHT SHE WAS LOOKING AT HER MOTHER.

When Rina had opened the door at 11 AM sharp, she was certain her mother stood there.

Her mother when she was young. Before she got married and had seven children and let her dreams fade. She saw a beautiful black woman wearing jeans and a black leather jacket, her straightened hair pulled from her face into a ponytail. She had shining brown eyes and a warm smile.

"Aren't you going to let me in?" Elin said with a laugh.

Rina took a step back and opened the door wider. "Yes, sorry." She'd expected a woman of mystery and intrigue, not this kind faced woman.

Elin sat down. "Thanks for seeing me. I know it wasn't easy." She looked in amazement at the bowl of barbecue potato chips Cirina had set on the coffee table. "You remembered."

"I wasn't sure they would still be your favorite," Rina said thinking of the meager chip packets they used to share as children.

She took a chip and grinned. "It is."

Rina sat down and rubbed her hands on her thighs. "What is this about? Why did you want to see me?"

"Sorry I've kept my distance this long, but I didn't have the courage to meet you." She sighed. "As you know our family comes with some baggage and I didn't want to be pulled into your life too."

"I don't want to be a burden—"

"That's not what I meant. I mean...I wasn't sure I could be the sister you needed. Or would even want. You grew up with Carla and Amelia while I was raised as an only child and I was happy with that. But then..." She shifted her gaze to the window and her voice grew soft. "I know what happened. Mom called me." Her gaze returned to Rina's face. "She didn't tell me everything but I put the pieces together and—"

"Oh, that," Rina said with a dismissive wave of her hand. "I'm going to fix it."

Elin narrowed her eyes. "There's nothing you need to fix. You don't owe anyone, anything. Let Amelia fail. Let Jenny be unhappy. I'm here to tell you that it's okay to walk away. That you won't be walking alone. I'm here for you. I spoke to Warren and he feels the same. You have a choice to make. You can keep trying to please everyone else or stop. It's up to you. If I am the only family you have left, will that be okay?"

Rina's heart pounded. This beautiful woman wanted to know her, be with her? It would be more than enough. For most of her life she'd felt torn between the Parkers and the Powells, but Elin was freeing her from both.

She didn't have to carry everyone's happiness. It wasn't her responsibility.

She was offering her a new life. A new family.

"Yes, it would."

Elin stood and held her arms open and Rina eagerly fell into them. "Then my dear sister," Elin said, holding her close. "You'll always have a home."

She had a beloved sister now, but over the next several weeks she sensed Warren growing distant. She noticed it even more over next few weeks.

He'd said he was fine with her decision not to help Amelia and not telling him about visiting her parents' apartment, but something else was bothering him.

He no longer touched her as he used to. There was still the light kiss, the tender brush of his fingers against her face, but it wasn't the same. Wasn't as playful. She feared she was losing him. She'd lost her family and the Parkers and only had Elin left. She didn't want to lose him too. She wanted him to know how much she care for him. She wanted to be useful to him. She pulled out all of Mr. CC's recipes, some that she'd tweaked over the years, and baked and cooked for him. But he didn't compliment her as he once had, he didn't gush over the dishes she prepared.

She didn't know what she was doing wrong. So she doubled her efforts, brushing aside his growing and insistent requests to eat with him. Twice, when she'd agreed to sit with him while he ate, he'd tried to feed her. She pushed his fork away and laughed, but she hated that. He even joked about how romantic it would be to eat from the same plate, which was a nightmarish thought. Why couldn't he just eat and enjoy the food and let her watch him? She didn't need food. Seeing him satisfied was all that mattered. She wanted him to know that he was safe, that she would always nourish him.

"Let me help you with the dishes," he said one evening. "You dry."

"No, I like doing them. Did you like dinner?"

"It was fine, but—"

That was all he would say recently. It was fine. Not amazing, not incredible. She was failing him. "I'll do better next time."

"Cirina, it's not that." He touched her shoulder, but his touch wasn't gentle. It was firm. "I need you to slow down. Did you eat today?"

"Of course." She didn't know. She couldn't remember if she ate today or yesterday or the day before. But she must have because she didn't feel hungry. She didn't need food like others did. She could get by without a lot. She didn't want him to worry. And he looked very worried. He didn't look at her the same way, with the same teasing affection he'd had only months ago.

Perhaps he was getting bored with her as his private chef. She needed to figure out what her next career move would be. But right now she needed to lie and make him feel better. She needed to figure out what he wanted her to say. "And I'll make us something to share for dessert tonight."

He nodded, released his hand from her shoulder, but she could tell that he didn't believe her.

She turned back to the dishes, her mind spinning. She scrubbed with all her might, she scrubbed as she was blinded by tears, she scrubbed until she felt as if her heart would burst out of her chest.

She scrubbed until she was overcome by darkness and couldn't scrub anymore.

CHAPTER THIRTY-NINE

The moment she opened her eyes, she knew where she was and the sight made her want to scream.

She was in a hospital.

How could she be in a hospital again?

She had to leave before Warren found out.

"Careful," a deep voice said.

She turned her head and saw Warren sitting by the side of her bed.

"You're in a hospital right now," he said in a gentle tone. She knew that tone. It was the tone the nurses and doctors had used with her. The studied, careful tone of concern and patronization. She didn't want to hear that voice from him.

"Was it another heart attack?"

"No, but—" He stopped and tried again. "You need help Cirina."

She sat up. "No, I don't. I promise. I'm sorry I caused any trouble."

He lowered his gaze. "You're dehydrated, malnourished—"

"I'm fine really." She reached for his hand. "Please believe me."

He lifted his gaze and his eyes met hers. They were filled with such sadness and pain that tears tightened her throat.

"You're not fine," Warren said. "But that doesn't stop me from loving you."

Rina felt the hot stream of tears slide down her face. "You love me?"

He nodded. "Yes." He tenderly cupped the side of her cheek. "So much that I'm not going to let you die. We're going to deal with this together."

"But I'm—"

His voice and gaze turned hard. "Cirina. Years ago you forced me to hear something I didn't want to. Now I'm going to do the same. You're not okay. You're not well. This could kill you and you have to do something about it."

"Please. Please don't send me away. I'll get better. I'll work hard, but I want to be with you." She didn't want to be alone again.

"I need you to make me a promise." He shook his head. "No, don't say anything, just listen." He took a deep breath. "We're going to leave the hospital and you're going to get counseling. If the counseling isn't enough...you will get inpatient care. No, I'm not finished."

Rina squeezed her eyes shut fighting against more tears.

"If you need inpatient care I want you to know your husband will be waiting for you."

She opened her eyes and gasped. "My husband?"

He nodded.

Her voice rose in surprise. "You'll marry me even though—"

"I'll marry you because I don't want to spend my life with anyone else. Because you're all I want and more. So do you agree?"

She hugged him. "Yes, I'll get better," she said in a choked voice. It was hard to admit she was sick, that she needed help, but she saw a future she wanted to be a part of. One she would fight for.

She stayed in the hospital a couple more days—more tests, more questions—but didn't resent them because Warren remained by her side.

She thought of how they'd met in a hospital so many years ago. How she'd followed him and watched him leave the hospital with his wife. How she'd wondered how it would feel to be cherished and loved.

As she was wheeled to the hospital exit she saw Elin standing by her car holding a smiley face balloon. She briefly felt the warmth of the bright sunshine of a spring afternoon, before Warren helped her into the back seat. She rested her head on his shoulder, her heart felt buoyant, her body full of peace.

She no longer had to imagine being a ghost, she no longer had to wonder what it was like to be loved.

She met her sister's gaze in the rear view mirror, felt

Warren's hand on top of hers and knew. She wasn't alone. She wasn't invisible.

She finally knew what it was like to love and be loved and it was the most heady feeling in the world.

CHAPTER FORTY

The beach house sat just steps from the Delaware Bay. Rina sat on the porch of the New Jersey house Warren had rented for the week and inhaled the scent of the water and soaked up the view while she finished the orange Warren had peeled for her. She'd taken advantage of the gourmet cookware in the fully equipped kitchen and had made them Caribbean rice and peas. They'd gone shopping in the quaint beach town and biked along the main drive aptly name Beach Avenue.

It had been almost four months since her trip to the hospital where she'd been diagnosed with a form of ARFID, otherwise known as Avoidant Restrictive Food Intake Disorder. Seven weeks since she'd started to see a counselor again, six weeks since Julian had agreed to sell Bee Sweet to her, five weeks since their private wedding. Warren's family (Rina's parents and siblings, except for her youngest brother and his girlfriend, hadn't been able to attend for various reasons. The Parkers refused to come), plus Steve and Elin had been in attendance, although Steve still didn't know Elin was the author of the books he wanted to license and she'd told Rina she wanted it to stay that way until she could find out more about him. But Rina secretly believed her sister didn't want Steve's excitement at meeting Elin to overshadow her wedding day. There would be time for a formal introduction at a later date.

Carla decided to quit the lab and study psychology to her parents' shock.

The Private Pastry Chef closed and Amelia started dating an exotic dancer shocking her parents even more than her sister had.

That's when Aunt Sonia's tirade began.

God sees all, and knows your dark heart.

You will prosper at nothing.

You're worthless.

You deserve nothing.

You're an ingrate.

The texts wouldn't stop coming. They flooded Rina's cell phone like toxic sludge.

No matter how she tried to block them, they managed to find a way through-twenty, sometimes fifty a day. Aunt Sonia was relentless.

One day Warren found Rina quickly tucking her phone in her back pocket when he entered the kitchen. "What are you doing?"

"I was trying a new recipe."

He frowned. "You're hiding something. What's going on?"

She shrugged and plastered on a grin. "Nothing. Actually, this new recipe—"

He held out his hand. "There are no secrets between us, remember?"

She reluctantly handed him the phone.

He quietly looked through the texts and nodded before he said, "I'll take care of this."

Rina breathed a sigh of relief. He wasn't angry. She'd been afraid if he knew he would do something drastic, but he was very calm. "Thank you. I've tried everything I can think of."

Warren slid the phone in his shirt pocket before he gently kissed her cheek, his lips warm when they touched her skin. "Use my phone until I get this sorted out."

She thought that was an inconvenience to him, but didn't want to argue. She'd take any help he could give her. The following day he said he wanted to take her on a drive to help get her mind off things.

She drove with the windows down letting the scent of freshly mowed lawns fill the car. She talked about how well her counseling sessions had gone, her plans for Bee Sweet and when she hoped to get started.

Rina lazed in pleasure until the scenery started to become familiar.

Too familiar.

She noticed the street where she used to walk as a child, the carefully orchestrated street path for pedestrians.

They were in Brandon.

Rina looked around panicked. "What are we doing

here?" Her heart began to pound as he turned the car onto the street where she'd grown up.

"It's time for me to talk to Aunt Sonia."

"No, you can't."

Warren parked his car in front of the elegant four level colonial and frowned at the expansive wraparound porch. His tone held a note of steel and his dark eyes met hers. "I can and I will."

She'd misjudged him. He hadn't been calm about the texts. He was angry. "You don't know what she's like. She hates me. She always has."

He opened the car door. "You don't have to come in with me if you don't want to. But this vendetta she has against you ends today." He stepped out and closed the door with enough force to make her flinch.

No, he wasn't angry. He was furious.

Rina raced after him and grabbed his arm. "It's bad enough that the Parkers blame me for Amelia's failed business. They also think I stole you away from her."

"Cirina." Warren covered her hand with his, before he removed her grip. "I don't care." He walked up to the door and rang the bell.

The housekeeper answered and stared at them in surprise.

"Who's at the door?" Aunt Sonia called from down the hall.

"Your niece Rina and a—"

"Don't let her in," Aunt Sonia said in a sharp tone. "Garbage should be left on the porch. Tell her I'll be there shortly."

Warren's eyes flashed fire. He grabbed Rina's hand,

pushed pass the housekeeper and found Aunt Sonia sitting in the great room with a book on her lap.

She stared up at him shocked. She took off her reading glasses and set them aside. "*You* have a nerve coming here." She looked past him and glared at Rina. "And you—what's this? Why are you here together?" She glanced down at their interlocked hands. "Flaunting your wanton ways. You are a vile—"

"And you are a parasite," Warren said in a soft voice.

Aunt Sonia blinked, briefly speechless. She wasn't used to anyone interrupting her. "I'm sorry?"

"What do you own? What do you do for a living? Have you done *anything* in the last thirty years?"

"I help my sister—"

"Like a leech you've been feeding off this family for years."

Sonia surged to her feet. "How dare you. I am a woman of God."

"I bet your hypocrisy makes Him laugh every day."

She took a step to walk past him. "I will not listen to this."

He blocked her path. "Yes, you will," he ground out between clenched teeth. "Sit down."

Her chilly glare met his. "And if I don't?"

"I will sue Amelia."

"What?"

He lifted a mocking brow. "Oh, she didn't tell you that she asked me for a loan? She was in such desperate need and I was eager to help her, but I am a businessman. I don't do anything without a lawyer. She hasn't paid me back yet."

Sonia slowly sunk into her seat. "You wouldn't."

Warren glanced at Rina, pensive. "I wonder if I should also add slander. She did try to ruin your reputation with the staff, right?"

"You won't win."

He shrugged. "Maybe, but it will be fun to try." He winked at the older woman. "I like playing games you know. I'm pretty good at them."

"What do you want?"

"To see you stripped naked and dragged over hot coals," he held up a hand when her eyes widened in horror, "but since that's unlikely to happen," he said with regret, "I have one simple request. You will never ever contact Cirina again. You will never speak to her again. Is that clear?"

She lowered her gaze.

"Otherwise, I'll also have to mention that tiny little gambling debt I covered for you."

Her head shot up.

"You didn't mind quietly asking Amelia's boyfriend for help. In exchange you would put in a good word for him with her parents since they listened to anything you told them. I believe those were your exact words." He clicked his tongue. "It would be such a pity if your sister found out that you hadn't really gone to a revival."

Her lips thinned.

"Do we understand each other now, Aunt Sonia?"

She released a deep breath and gave a curt nod.

"Good and I'd start praying for your own soul, if I were you." Warren took Rina's hand and walked out.

Aunt Sonia hadn't bothered her since that day.

Soon after the confrontation with Aunt Sonia, Warren said he wanted to take her away for a little while. She'd never expected the beautiful beach house and how much she'd needed to get away from all that had happened.

Rina left the porch and walked along the beach until the sunset started to cast long shadows on the ground.

She heard the voice of man with a West Indian accent telling people about a fudge shop located on the main road. "The best you've ever tasted," he said. She turned and saw a man of Asian heritage handing a girl a pamphlet. "Come by for a sweet treat. My name is Charlie Chin, but you can call me Mr. Charlie or CC."

Rina felt her body tremble. She couldn't believe it. At first she started to jog closer, then she started to run. The years had added a slight stoop to his back, some grey to his black hair and wrinkles to his face, but he was still the same.

"Mr. CC!"

He spun around.

She tapped her chest. "It's me Rina. Rina Powell. I used to help you—"

"I know," he said with a twinkle in his eyes. "I may be old but my memory is as sharp as ever." He looked her up and down. "But this big grown girl cannot be my little Rina dressed so fine."

"I became a pastry chef. I never forgot you. I never got to thank you for all you did for me. I've missed you so much. I still have your recipes and—" She stopped, when he pulled out a piece of cake from his pocket and held it out to her. She noticed the coconut treat and its pink hue topping.

"You still like grater cake?" he said.

She took the cake from him and popped it in her mouth. "I love grater cake," she said her heart full of joy. She pointed to the cottage where she knew Warren would be composing in the living room. She'd told him about Mr. CC and now she had the chance for the two most important men in her life to meet each other. "Come. Let me make you something delicious."

ABOUT THE AUTHOR

Dara Girard, an award-winning, national bestselling author of more than forty novels, from romance to suspense, loves telling stories.

Born in the US to immigrant parents, Dara enjoys pulling from her Jamaican, British, Nigerian heritage and exposure to various cultures to bring what reviewers and fans call "vivid emotional stories" to life. She is best known for her popular Henson Series, the mysterious Clifton Sisters, and the fun Black Stockings Society.

You can write her at:

contactdara@daragirard.com

or

P.O. Box 10345

Silver Spring, MD 20914

If you'd like to receive a reply, please send a self-addressed stamped envelope.

Visit her website to sign up for her newsletter and get sneak peeks, monthly updates on new releases, and special offers.

For more information visit
www.daragirard.com